W9-BZC-593

THE GHOST OF SCHAFER MEADOWS

THE GHOST OF SCHAFER MEADOWS

BETH HODDER

The Ghost of Schafer Meadows

by Beth Hodder

Copyright ©2007

All rights reserved. This book is protected under the copyright laws of the United States of America. No part of this book may be reproduced in any form or by any electronic or mechanical means including information storage and retrieval systems without permission in writing from the publisher, except by a reviewer, who may quote brief passages in a review.
Published by Grizzly Ridge Publishing, P.O. Box 268, West Glacier, MT 59936.

10 9 8 7 6 5 4 3 2 1

ISBN 978-0-9793963-0-4

Printed in the United States of America

Library of Congress Control Number: 2007903727

Attention schools, colleges and universities, corporations, and writing and publishing organizations: Quantity discounts are available on bulk purchases of this book for educational training purposes, fund-raising, or gift giving. For information contact Marketing Department, Grizzly Ridge Publishing, P.O. Box 268, West Glacier, MT 59926

Cover Illustration by Maria Vekkos

Map of Schafer Meadows by Guy Zoellner

Design and Typesetting by Donna Collingwood

Manuscript Editing by Florence Ore

For more information: www.grizzlyridgepublishing.com

This is a work of fiction. Names and characters in this novel are the product of the author's imagination, or, if real, are used fictitiously without any intent to describe their actual conduct. Institutions and places in this novel are real. However, the political and administrative settings of this novel are not meant to represent the actual policies of any institution or law enforcement agency.

For Al

In memory of Ruth Hodder, mother and friend, who believed
I could do it

In memory of Penny and Jasper

Acknowledgements

As I wrote this book, I was overwhelmed by the generosity of so many people who gave freely of their ideas, time, and talents.

I would like to thank the following people who read the manuscript and offered suggestions that helped me improve the book: Rose Beranek, Mollie Boisen, Danielle Crandell, Ann DeSimone, Lynne Dixon, Sylvia Eisenmann, Helen Gallagher, Bryan, Sherri, and Bill Haag, Heidi Haugen, Don Halloran, Victor Murphy, Deb Mucklow, Vivian Rosenthal, Shannon Sommers, Lauren and Aleisa Stevens, Thad Wollan, Joan and Mark Wierzba.

Two Columbia Falls, MT School District Six classes also read and provided important critiques for this book. I thank Doris Guidi and class and Julie Moylan and class for helping me in this endeavor.

Terry Divoky, Columbia Falls School District Six librarian, encouraged teachers to have their classes read and critique the manuscript.

Lorney "Jay" Deist provided me with information and folklore about William Schafer.

Sylvia Stearns proofread the manuscript.

Special Thanks

I would like to give special thanks to the following people:

My husband, Al Koss, for the time, space, encouragement, love, and support to write this book and for help with editing and proofreading.

Janet Muirhead Hill, author of the award-winning *Miranda and Starlight Series* of horse stories, for insights into the world of book publishing.

Florence Ore, whose advice and encouragement answered my many questions and strengthened the story.

Marian Strange, "leetle seester" and incredible editor, whose red pen tightened my wandering prose. Mom would have been proud.

Marjorie J. Fisher, author of *A Business of My Own? 21 Steps to starting and running a successful small business*, who led me through the entire process as mentor and friend.

Mary McNeill and Maxine Watkinds, two people with extraordinary talent and huge hearts. They took me, a total stranger, into their home and spent hours critiquing this book, challenging my thinking and giving me the courage to face the troll and walk past it. From them I learned the importance of kindness, generosity, and friendship.

Table of Contents

ONE

Spotted Bear Ranger Station

"Great! Just great!" I said to Oriole, loud enough for Mom and Dad to hear. "For this we left our home and friends in New Mexico?"

Oriole looked up at me, her black ear and eye cocked to the side as if wondering what was wrong.

Dad's job with the U.S. Forest Service moved our family all over the country. This time he dragged us to Montana, about as far north from New Mexico as you could get. We might as well have moved to the other side of the world as far as I was concerned.

We'd just arrived at the Spotted Bear Ranger Station, where my dad had to report for his newest job. From there we'd go to our summer home at the Schafer Meadows Ranger Station within the Great Bear Wilderness.

"Look at this place," I said to my tall, lanky 16-year-old brother. "It's disgusting. If Schafer Meadows is anything like Spotted Bear, I'm gonna die there."

Jed bent down to Oriole and scratched her yellow ear. The brim on Jed's ever-present black cowboy hat hid his blue eyes and black hair. "I don't know, Jessie. Looks pretty cool to me. You're just mad because we had to move again. But if our home in Silver City had looked like this, you'd love it here."

"What do you mean? Spotted Bear's just a bunch of old log cabins at the end of a dusty gravel road miles from nowhere. Talk about primitive. And look at these mountains. See that white stuff up there? It's snow—snow! That means cold. I miss the desert."

"Jessie, won't you even give it a chance?" Dad's dark eyes showed the pain I had put there.

"Come on, Dad, think about it—there aren't many 12-year-old girls who get stuck living in a wilderness. And only adults work at Schafer Meadows. How will I make friends?"

"You always make friends easily, honey. The folks at Schafer may not be your age, but I know they'll like you right away. And don't forget you've got Oriole. You've met a lot of people because of her."

"Yeah, well, Oriole's all I've got now. You've taken me away from my home and my best friends. What could be worse?"

A gust of wind blew Mom's silky blonde hair. She pushed it away from her face and looked at me through blue eyes. "It won't be that terrible if you try."

"Oh, yes it will. Once we go into the wilderness there won't be any TV, cell phone coverage, Internet, cement for skateboarding—nothing. We won't even have electricity. How isolated can you get? We'll lose all touch with civilization."

The tears came close to spilling over. Nobody cared how I felt—not Dad, Mom, not even Jed. I swallowed a lump in my throat.

I was on a roll and ready to let out more of my anger when we reached a long natural-colored log building that said "office" on the outside. We stood just inside the door. A young woman with curly brown hair sat at a desk behind a counter. Maps filled the wall behind her and a giant grizzly bear hide hung high above them. A Forest Service radio squawked. Through the static we heard a man call Spotted Bear. The woman grabbed the microphone and talked back. She smiled, waved us into the office, and raised a finger, indicating that she'd be with us shortly.

Finally she finished her conversation. "Sorry about that. We have no phone service in the wilderness, so the radio is our main communication line. There's something going on with law enforcement, and I had to relay some messages. How may I help you?"

"I'm Tom Scott, the new ranger at Schafer Meadows," Dad said. "This is my wife, Kate, son, Jed, and daughter, Jessie."

The woman stood up and came around the desk, extending her hand. "Oh, hi, Tom. Glad to meet you. I've heard lots about you and your family."

She shook all of our hands. "And I'm Cindy Miller. You'll probably hear me on the radio a lot this summer when you're back at Schafer Meadows. I'm so envious of you going to live there. It's a great place—one of the best—beautiful and wild. It even has a resident ghost."

By the look on her face, I could tell she thought she had said the wrong thing, but as if to cover up her mistake, she shrugged and said, "Hey, doesn't every place have a ghost?"

I was about to ask what she meant when a whine came from outside. I hurried to the door. "Sorry. The whiner is my dog, Oriole."

"Oh, I love dogs," Cindy said as she walked to the door to look out. She went outside and stooped to scratch Oriole's ears. Oriole's back leg involuntarily scratched in response. "Look at those marks on her. She's beautiful. What kind of dog is she?"

I smiled down at Oriole, whose shiny light yellow coat contrasted sharply with her black left eye and ear and black chest. "Hard to say. Dad got her for me from the animal shelter this past winter when she was only eight weeks old. They think her mother might have been a Labrador or golden retriever. Maybe she got the black color from a German shepherd or hound of some sort."

"Interesting. With your brownish blonde hair and brown eyes, you two compliment each other well. How'd she get her name?"

I grinned. "Mom and I love to watch birds, and I thought my puppy looked a lot like a Hooded Oriole—you know—yellow, with black markings on her face, ear, and neck.
She was such a tiny thing, kind of like a bird. And her little voice warbled like one. She'd go 'Rooooo.' So I named her Oriole."

"Smart?"

"The smartest. She learns most things fast, many after the first try." I bent down to pat her head. "She's the best."

"Well, she's sure sweet. You can bring her to visit me anytime."

"What's up with the law enforcement problem?" Jed asked.

"It's not really a problem—not here anyway. Some of the sheriff's deputies are camping and fishing in the wilderness for the weekend, and the sheriff is trying to reach them. I'm not sure why. Might be some trouble in Kalispell or something. Let me get the district ranger—the boss—for you."

A dark-haired woman wearing a sage green Forest Service uniform and cowboy boots stuck out her hand in Dad's direction. "Hi, Tom. I'm Rosie Anderson."

Rosie looked about the same age as Mom and Dad. I'm only 5'0" and 85 pounds, but she didn't look like she weighed much more than me. I wondered how she could handle the hard physical work she'd have to do in this remote place.

Taking us all in, she smiled. "Welcome to Spotted Bear. How was your trip?"

"Good," Dad said. "Everything went without a hitch. And the drive was spectacular."

We must have been on different trips, I thought as I glared at Dad. We drove for five long, horrible days pulling a large horse trailer packed with hay and our belongings. Oriole hogged the back seat, so Jed and I sat pinned against the doors most of the way. We had to unload the mule and four horses from the trailer a couple of times a day, water them, and shovel manure. Talk about stink! Whooee! Oriole needed exercise, too, and I had to watch her carefully in areas of heavy traffic. All this work made my muscles scream, and the four of us looked like we'd not had a shower in a month—probably smelled like it, too.

"Well, I'm glad you made it here safely," Rosie said. "I'm sure you're plenty tired after your long trip. Would you like to rest or are you up for a tour of the ranger station?"

After driving so long we were glad to be standing, so we opted for the tour. Oriole raced around, sniffing everything in sight, as if also happy to be out of the car.

Spotted Bear looked like a small old western town surrounded by high mountains. As we slowly walked, Rosie pointed out log buildings, some from the 1920s, all painted dark brown with white-trimmed windows. There were bunkhouses for crews and a big cookhouse for large groups and meetings. We also saw a couple of larger brown frame houses. Rosie pointed to one.

"When you're at Spotted Bear you'll live in that house along the river," Rosie said. "There'll be plenty of room for the four of you and Oriole. Oh, hey! Here are a couple of people I want you to meet."

A boy and girl about my age walked toward us. I couldn't take my eyes off them. The boy, close to my height, had sandy brown hair. The girl was tall and dark-haired. She wore thin round glasses.

Rosie called them over. "Jessie, this is Will Lightner. His dad works here. And this is Allie Carter, a friend of Will's. They'll both go to school with you this fall."

All of a sudden I felt shy. Will was even cuter than Johnny Ricardo from my seventh grade class in Silver City, New

Mexico, and Allie looked really friendly. I couldn't seem to say anything. Finally, Will spoke.

"Hey, Jessie. Rosie told Allie and me you were coming."

Somehow I found my voice. "Yeah, well, glad to meet you."

"Maybe I'll get to see you this summer at Schafer Meadows. Dad sometimes goes there and takes me along."

"Yeah, I'd like that a lot."

"Mind if we tag along?"

"That'd be great."

My luck seemed to be changing. It might not be so lonely here after all.

"Cool dog," Allie said. "Can I pet her?"

"Sure. She loves people."

Will threw a stick for Oriole. "I've got a dog that would probably get along great with your dog."

"I hope they can meet soon. Oriole needs a playmate, too."

Both Allie and Will played with Oriole as we walked along.

Rosie stopped at a tall two-story log building. "Crew leaders live here when they're not in the wilderness."

She took us down a small hill to a door in the basement. Unlocking the door, she said, "This is the food cache."

"You need cash for food?" I asked. "Why?"

Rosie shook her head. "Guess I need to explain. 'Cash' means money, but a 'cache'—pronounced the same way—is a place to store things. We needed somewhere to keep all our produce and dry goods, so we turned the basement into a food cache."

"Wait'll you see this place," Will said. "It's huge."

"Why's it so big?" I asked.

"You can't just go around the corner to get a gallon of milk or a candy bar or something. The closest grocery store's about two hours away."

"Right," Rosie said. "So we have to keep lots of food on hand. We supply all the groceries for the wilderness crews and keep the backcountry cabins and ranger stations stocked with basic supplies. This cache acts like a cellar where we keep food until it's ready to be taken into the wilderness."

Rosie opened the door. "Come on in."

"Wow," Jed said as we walked in. "It's like a small store. I can't believe all the food—canned, boxed, even fresh and frozen. There's everything in here." Jed has a big appetite, so this made him very happy.

"Told you it was big," Will said.

"And look at all the nuts, grains, beans, pasta, and other dry goods," Mom said. "This is impressive."

"You'll get your groceries for Schafer from here," Rosie said.

Allie picked up a jar of grape jelly. "Once I got to watch the packers bundle the food. They had to wrap everything like this jelly jar really well so nothing got damaged or broken when the mule strings took it into Schafer."

"Our food comes in on mules?" I asked. "Why?"

Will laughed. "You can't drive to Schafer. There aren't any roads in the wilderness—only trails. Without the pack strings you'd have to carry everything yourself."

"No way. It'd take us all summer just to haul our food and gear."

"It would," Rosie said. "So the mules do the work for you. Some of our mules carry as much as 200 pounds on their backs. We tie nine of the big critters to each other in a single file string with one person or 'packer' leading them up a trail. Believe me, you'll be grateful to see eggs arrive unbroken after riding for 20 miles in a pack on the back of a mule. Those long-ears have even carried in refrigerators."

"I can't imagine a refrigerator riding down a trail on a mule. That must be something to see."

"Want to see the barn?"

"Thanks," Dad said to Rosie, "but we can probably take it from here. I think we've gotten a pretty good feel for the ranger station. Maybe we should let you go and we can unload our animals and move into our house."

"That sounds great, Tom. I need to get back and contact the sheriff's office and get a few other things done before the end of the day. You can keep your horses and mule in the corral until you go to Schafer."

To Jed and me she said, "Make sure you go down to the South Fork of the Flathead River. I think you'll find it pretty interesting. The South Fork runs behind your house."

We were walking away when Will said, "Hey, Jessie. Want to come with me and Allie to my house? You can bring Oriole."

I looked between Dad and Mom. "Can I go?"

"Sure," Dad said. "We'll meet you at the house later. Have fun."

Will's cabin was small with a steeply peaked roof and a lot of fancy decorations or "gingerbread" on the outside. As we entered, Will said, "My mom died when I was eight, so I live here with just my dad and Casey."

The downstairs had a small living room, kitchen, and bathroom. A narrow spiral staircase led up to a loft. We all climbed the stairs. Two beds and two dressers filled the wall space. A dog bed lay on the floor next to one bed. Oriole sniffed the bed all over, wagging her tail.

"Is Casey your brother?" I asked.

"No, he's our dog. Dad uses him for law enforcement work. He's great. I'm sure he and Oriole will have lots of fun together."

"Where are your dad and Casey now?"

"Dad got called out this morning and won't be back until later today."

"Maybe we can meet them when they get back."

"Not this time. As soon as Dad gets back we have to leave for some meeting he has in Kalispell."

"Oh, well. Another time. You'll be around, though, won't you, Allie?"

Allie shook her head. "My family's camped at the Spotted Bear Campground and we're leaving this afternoon."

"Bummer." I looked at the ground. There went my ideas for fun.

Will saw the look on my face. "Hey. There'll be plenty of time this summer for the three of us to get together."

"Yeah, right." I wondered how often anyone would go as far back in the wilderness as Schafer Meadows just to visit. "Well, guess it's time to see our house."

Getting Oriole to walk up the spiral staircase in Will's house was easy. Getting her down took some work. Looking down must have frightened her, because she took the first two steps and then backed up. I was behind her. She nearly knocked me off my feet trying to return to the loft. I gently nudged her back end to start her down the stairs again and then had to coax her step by step as she slowly wound her way toward the first floor. She wrinkled her brow, panted hard, and licked her lips, looking tortured. About halfway down she relaxed a bit, and by the time she hit the bottom step, her tail wagged once more.

I followed her into the living room. She turned around and raced back up the stairs.

"Oh, no!" I said. "You're not going to make me do that all over again?"

But Oriole spiraled down the stairs as fast as her four legs could carry her. She had found a new and interesting game.

Allie laughed. "Your dog's nuts. Is she always like this?"

"She has her moments, especially when trying something new. Guess she just couldn't resist."

We laughed as Oriole raced up and down the stairs two more times, obviously having a great time.

"I hate to leave, but we'd better be going," I finally said. "Hope to see both of you soon. Come visit us at Schafer if you can."

"Can't wait," Allie said. She was still talking as the door closed behind Oriole and me. I heard her say, "Will said there's a pretty active ghost back there."

I opened the door again. "What?"

Will grinned. "You'll see."

The Swimming Hole

Mom was poking around in the house. It had a large kitchen, storage room, dining room, living room with a big picture window, three bedrooms, and a bathroom. It was furnished, so all we needed was food, bedding, and our own belongings.

"Hey, Mom, can I have the bedroom off the living room?"

"Check with Jed, but if he doesn't care, it's fine with me."

Dad and Jed arrived right then. As it turned out, Jed liked the bedroom next to Mom and Dad's, so Oriole and I moved into ours. Oriole slept on my bed, but I kept a foam pad with a blanket on it next to the bed for times when she wanted her own space. I hung a few pictures on the wall of June and Julie, the Two J's, my best friends from New Mexico. Then I was ready to explore some more.

"Can Oriole and I go down to the river?"

"Sure," Mom said. "Just be careful. Rosie said the South Fork can move pretty fast this time of year."

Jed came along. The three of us went out the door and followed a trail close to the river. We came to an abrupt edge above the river, which was over a hundred feet wide. A long swinging bridge spanned the water.

"Wow!" Jed said. "This must be what Rosie meant when she said we'd find the river interesting. Let's check it out."

Jed and I ran to a path that led to the bridge. Oriole sniffed around behind us but soon caught up and raced past us.

Suddenly she stopped. The bridge was made of long wooden boards. Heavy cables supported the sides. Four-foot high wire mesh ran the length of it, so we couldn't fall off.

The bridge was sturdy, but the whole thing swayed, up, down, and sideways, and we could see clear to the river, 20 or 30 feet below us. Oriole had never seen anything like it, and she froze with fear. She looked more scared than she had on Will's staircase.

"It's okay, girl," I told her. "It's safe to walk on. Watch me." I walked around her and moved about ten feet in front to coax her. "Come on, Oriole."

She started forward but stopped the moment the bridge began to move. "Come on," I called. Oriole took a few steps but then turned around and headed to the end of the bridge and the safety of land. Jed was there, and he stopped her from running back up the hill.

"Tell you what," he said. "Get her started toward you again. I'll stay behind her so she can't go back. We'll just take it slow so she doesn't get too spooked." He turned her toward me.

When I called her this time, she timidly got onto the boards. She crouched, all four feet splayed out, the nails on all four paws digging into the boards. "Come on Oriole," I said softly. "It's all right. We won't let you get hurt."

As she inched forward, Jed inched behind her. We made slow but steady progress until we were about halfway across the bridge. Then all of a sudden, as if nothing had happened out of the ordinary, Oriole stood erect, pulled in her claws, got her legs under her, and trotted past me to the other side of the bridge with her head held high. She stood wagging her tail until Jed and I caught up to her.

Jed shook his head. "I can't believe what I've just seen."

"She's a fast learner. Always has been. Now that she's crossed it once, she'll be fine on the bridge."

We found a sandy beach on the other side of the river. The icy water cooled all thoughts of swimming, but a group of eight people sunbathed. They laughed at something and waved to us. I was surprised to see them. I wondered if they worked at Spotted Bear.

Oriole had learned to swim in New Mexico and took to it from the start. We went a little upriver from the sunbathers to toss a few sticks in the water for her to retrieve.

"This will be great exercise for her." Oriole swam after a stick Jed threw, grabbing it in her mouth and slapping her tail on the water like a beaver as she turned to bring it back to us.

Stepping out of the river, soaked and dripping, she held the stick in her mouth and shook herself. Water sprayed in every direction. Jed and I let out war whoops as we jumped back to keep the cold water from soaking us.

Jed threw the stick a little farther out, and Oriole paddled after it. The stick entered some rapids, and she swam into the current, intent on retrieving it.

"Oriole! No!" I cried.

It was too late. Oriole caught the stick at the same time she hit the rapids. She swam with all her might, but the rushing river carried her quickly downstream, bobbing like a cork. A large rock caught one shoulder and spun her around, banging her hard on the head. She thrashed about, still paddling and holding onto the stick, barely staying above water. Then suddenly her head dropped. She stopped struggling.

The swift current carried Oriole's limp body downstream. She started to sink. I chased after her at the water's edge.

"Help! Someone!"

One of the sunbathers closer to her than Jed or I saw what was happening, ran to the water, dove in, and grabbed her just as she reached an even faster current. Somehow he hung on to her collar and pulled her to shore.

Oriole lay on her side, her soaked coat clinging to her. She had stopped breathing. I dropped to my knees. Tears rolled down my face and splashed onto her beautiful yellow fur.

By this time a small group of people had gathered around us. Someone leaned over and put a hand on Oriole's side. From what seemed far away, I heard a man's voice say, "She's got a heartbeat." Then large, gentle hands pushed on Oriole's chest.

It only took one push. Oriole coughed, sputtering water from her mouth. Her large brown eyes opened and she took big gulps of air. Her tail thumped, slowly at first and then faster. The next thing I knew, she was on her feet, reaching for the stick that she had somehow clung to throughout the rescue.

"Oh, Oriole," I squeaked. "I thought you were dead."

I grabbed her, giving her a huge bear hug of relief. She wagged her tail and licked my face. Then she wriggled free from my grip and raced to the river, dropping the stick so we could throw it again.

"You've got quite the determined dog there," said our rescuer.

I looked at him for the first time. He was about 25 years old and over six feet tall, with brown eyes and dark brown hair that reached to his ears. Water dripped from his hair, nose, and chin. Goosebumps covered his muscular arms and legs and he shivered. One of the women onlookers put a large beach towel around his shoulders. He hugged it tightly.

Still barely able to speak, I finally stammered, "Thank you…thank you so much!"

He nodded, smiled, and ran his hands down his face like a squeegee to wipe the water away. Oriole came over and he knelt next to her. She wagged her tail and leaned her soggy body against him.

Jed sat on the sand behind us, pale and staring. I leaned over and put my hand on his arm. "Jed, it's all right. It wasn't your fault. You didn't know the river would be so strong."

"Yes, I did," he mumbled, taking off his cowboy hat and dropping his eyes to the ground. "Mom told us to be careful. I could have killed Oriole."

Our rescuer stood next to Jed. "In remote areas like Spotted Bear you always have to be aware of what's happening around you. Take anything for granted and you can get into trouble fast." He reached out a hand to help Jed up. "But I bet you'll be more careful from now on."

"No kidding," Jed said, looking a little less pale. "By the way, I'm Jed Scott, and this is my kid sister, Jessie. Our dad's the new ranger at Schafer Meadows. Who are you?"

He smiled and wiped more water from his face. "Pete Randolph. I'm the assistant ranger at Schafer Meadows. I'll be your dad's right-hand man. Looks like we'll see a lot of each other this summer."

I looked up at Pete, unable to stop grinning. What luck to have found someone so willing to just jump in and help. Plus it didn't hurt that he was really cute. And he'd be at Schafer all summer. At that moment I felt like I'd found my new best friend.

A sudden screech from one of the sunbathers made us look in their direction. A soaking wet, very happy yellow and black bundle of fur stood in the middle of the group, shaking herself from the tip of her nose to the end of her tail, spraying water all over everyone.

Jed laughed. "That's Jessie's dog, Oriole. You'll see lots of her this summer, too. Hopefully not because she's in more trouble."

"We'd better get back home," I said to Jed, whistling for Oriole to come. "We might have a murder on our hands if one of those wet sunbathers wants to get even with Oriole."

"Thanks again," I said to Pete as we left. "I owe you one."

Oriole raced across the bridge, grinning at us from the other side.

THREE

Schafer Meadows

Dad and Jed left for Schafer Meadows with the trail crew to spend a week opening the ranger station while Mom and I stayed behind at Spotted Bear. I called New Mexico every day and talked with my best friends, the Two J's, knowing it would be a long time before we could do it again. I also wrote them a couple of letters, trying to ward off my homesickness. Finally Dad and Jed came for us.

We left on a Saturday. Brad Peters, the main Schafer packer, had left early in the morning before us with his mule string, carrying all the gear we thought we might need for the summer.

My horse, Red, was the last in the trailer, so I unloaded him first when we got to the trailhead. He backed out easily, feeling for the end of the trailer with one back hoof before taking the first step down to the ground. Once out, I tied him to the side of the trailer, brushed him, put his saddle blanket on, set the saddle on his back, and cinched it tightly. He took the bridle bit in his mouth and then stood waiting patiently. I rolled up my raincoat and tied it to the saddle. Then I put my lunch, water, and Oriole's treats in my saddlebags and dusted off my brown cowboy boots and white straw cowboy hat, knowing they'd soon be covered in dust again. Mom, Dad, and Jed finished saddling their horses and our mule, Kitty, who carried what trip gear we didn't have in our saddlebags. We were ready to go.

When we started out on the trail, Oriole scouted ahead with me riding behind her. Red's brown coat shone in the sun and his black mane flowed as the breeze picked up.

Occasionally Oriole would stop and let out a "Roooooo!" She sounded happy and excited. Mom followed me on Smurf, her small dapple gray horse. Jed rode behind Mom on Rocky, Red's brother who looked like his twin. Dad took up the rear, riding his buckskin Dillon and leading Kitty, our black mule.

As we rode up the Big Bill Trail, Dad said, "You know, Schafer Meadows is in the Great Bear Wilderness, part of what's called the 'Bob Marshall Wilderness Complex.' The Great Bear, Bob Marshall, and Scapegoat wildernesses together total more than one and a half million acres. That's larger than the whole state of Delaware. Pretty big if you ask me."

We reached the top of the ridge and rounded a bend in the trail. A huge basin spread out before us filled with hundreds and hundreds of tall white flowers rising from what looked like large tufts of grass. The ground looked covered with snow.

"What are those?" I asked.

"Lilies," Dad said. "They're called beargrass. Aren't they incredible? I don't know why they're called that. Bears don't eat the flowers or their bulbs."

We rode through a sea of beargrass until we reached a large wooden sign that marked the entrance to the Great Bear Wilderness. Excitement hit us all, and we talked and laughed and stopped to look at the scenery.

Dad smiled. "Welcome to your new home." The wind ruffled his black hair. Sitting astride Dillon with such ease, his medium frame leaning on his saddle horn, Dad looked so much like the wilderness ranger he was—like he belonged there. All I could think was, *now we'll never go back to New Mexico.*

"Look around you. Look at this!"

I looked around. Mountain peaks filled the skyline. New Mexico's mountains were mostly hilly and open, with well-spaced shrubs and short oak trees or towering ponderosa pines. These mountains had jagged peaks and were covered with evergreen trees.

"Boy, I wouldn't want to have to go off trail in this country," Mom said. "The trees and shrubs are thick in there. You'd have a terrible time getting through them."

"What kind of trees are those, Dad?" Jed asked.

"The large ones are mostly Douglas-fir and spruce. The small, straight ones are lodgepole pine."

"That's a funny name."

"They're called that because Native Americans used them to make poles for their teepees or lodges."

Whitcomb Peak towered over us, not thick and green like the other mountains but rocky and open. A few small crystal-clear streams crossed the trail, gurgling down the mountainside. Oriole had plenty of chances to get a cold drink as she trotted along.

"Hard to believe there can still be snow in late June," Mom said as we carefully guided our horses over slick patches of heavy wet snow left in Whitcomb's shadow.

Jed laughed and pointed. "Look at your crazy dog, Jessie."

Oriole had never seen snow before. She sniffed it before gingerly walking on it like it was fragile and would break. She slipped and flopped on her belly, sliding downhill about five feet. Looking startled but pleased, she jumped up and ran back to the trail, got down on her stomach with all four legs spread out, burrowed her face in the snow, and slid straight downhill again.

She dropped a stick in the snow and pounced on it with her front paws, burying it. Then she furiously dug and dug in the snow until her head disappeared like an ostrich and her back end stuck up in the air with her tail wagging wildly. When she retrieved her stick she raced ahead with her trophy.

"I hope there's not a lot more snow on the trail to Schafer Meadows," I said, shaking my head. "It'll take us days to get there at the rate Oriole's going. She's having way too much fun."

The trail was about 20 miles long, and Oriole ran up and back, up and back, sticking her nose between rocks, looking for any sign of rodents. Later when we started down Schafer Creek and huge trees hovered over the trail, she kept us safe by barking away any squirrels that had the nerve to cross our path.

Dad inhaled deeply. "I love the crisp clean scent of pine and fir. Nothing makes me feel more alive."

I felt that way, too, but Dad didn't need to know that right now. Instead, I ignored him and birded with Mom. A grouse shot up from the trail like an explosion and flew off. Its wings drummed such a racket that it scared us all to death. Panicked, I jumped in my saddle, Mom gave a startled "eek," Dad ducked, and Jed pulled his heels into Rocky's side so hard that Rocky thought Jed wanted him to run. It took some work on Jed's part to calm him down. We all had a good laugh when we realized everyone was fine.

The grouse perched in a shrub next to the trail, so Mom and I got a good look at it. The bold, dark bars on its flanks and the dark tail band identified it as a Ruffed Grouse. They didn't live in New Mexico, so we excitedly added a new bird to our lists.

As we neared Schafer, we had to cross some clear streams. I still worried about Oriole in water after her near drowning in the South Fork River. She waded through the streams with no problem, but as we neared our final crossing, the Middle Fork of the Flathead River, my unease increased.

We heard the river before seeing it. The water sounded fast and dangerous. I felt the blood drain from my face as I remembered Oriole lying limp as the raging river carried her downstream. But when we came out of the trees to the water's edge, it didn't look as bad as I feared.

"Why don't Oriole and I go last so we can see how deep and fast it is?"

The water reached to Smurf's belly when Mom took

him across. Smurf's a short horse—I can almost see over his back—but he's still way taller than Oriole.

They crossed the river easily, and Dad waited for us on the other side, letting Dillon and Kitty drink at the water's edge.

I took a deep breath. "Okay, let's go, Oriole."

We started out together. She hit the water and immediately had to swim. I panicked as the river started to carry her downstream, but she turned upstream to face the current and easily swam across. I let out a huge sigh of relief. She was safe. I knew the river wouldn't be a problem this summer.

A quarter mile after crossing the Middle Fork, Jed stopped.

"Hey look—a campground."

The small campground with a few picnic tables was nestled among some small lodgepole pine trees. Beyond the campground we saw a wooden pole corral, a barn, and a grassy airstrip with a couple of small planes. Past the barn were some old log buildings. We had reached the Schafer Meadows Ranger Station and our new summer home.

A short stocky man with arms bulging against his faded white T-shirt worked next to the barn. He turned when he saw us coming and took off his cowboy hat, revealing brown hair.

"Hey, how's it going? Good to see all of you."

He wiped his hand on his jeans before reaching for Dad's hand. Dad leaned down from his saddle and took it.

"Nice to be here at last. Kate, Jessie, you remember Brad Peters, the Schafer packer?" Dad said to us. We nodded and shook hands with Brad.

"Glad you made it here safely. Your gear arrived in good shape."

Brad went back to unpacking wooden boxes wrapped in "manty" tarps made of heavy white canvas. They held the supplies the mules had carried on their backs to Schafer. Brad handed me a package.

"Your friend, Allie, asked me to give this to you."

I grinned. The grape jelly jar Allie had picked up in the food cache at Spotted Bear came with a note wrapped around it held by a rubber band.

Dear Jessie,

Did the jar arrive unbroken? Aren't the mules and Packer Brad amazing? Didn't you love the ride in? Write to me and tell me all about your trip. Hope to see you soon.

Your friend,

Allie

P.S. Will says hi and watch out for the ghost!

Wow! She signed it "Your friend, Allie." It felt good to have a friend already. Two friends. I laughed off the joke about the ghost.

We rode on to the cookhouse to unload the manties from Kitty. A familiar figure came out from the cookhouse basement.

"Hey Pete," I said, recognizing Oriole's rescuer. "How goes it?"

I jumped off Red and hugged Pete. My legs almost gave out after riding in the saddle for so long.

"Everything's great." Pete hugged me back and began to untie the ropes holding one side of Kitty's manties. "How was your trip?"

"Wonderful," Mom said. "The country's beautiful and Jessie and I saw a new bird. No animals except squirrels, though."

We looked up at the large two-story log cookhouse. Dark brown with green and white trim along the windows, it looked a lot like some of the old buildings at Spotted Bear. Maybe I was getting used to those old buildings, because they didn't look so disgusting to me now. I've always hated it when Jed was right. Maybe I was still mad at Dad for making us move and just didn't want to admit it.

We tied up our horses, and about that time two people came around the corner of the cookhouse to meet us.

"We'll give you a hand unloading," said Celie Long Runner, a Native American from the Blackfeet Nation just outside the wilderness boundary. Her real name is Celeste, but she prefers Celie, pronounced like Seeley Lake, a town nearby. We had met at Spotted Bear. Tall and thin, Celie's leanness hid sheer strength—strength she needed as the trail crew leader. All the guys at Spotted Bear drooled over her and her high cheekbones, dark smooth skin, and long black hair worn in a single braid. I liked her because she made me feel like a friend. Guess I had more friends than I realized.

Cody Gray, a member of Celie's trail crew, also helped us unload. Like the other trail crew members, Cody was about 20. He was built a lot like Jed and had the same ever-present cowboy hat worn with the brim facing down.

"Whoa. What's that smell?" Jed asked. The aroma of roast beef floated our way from upstairs in the cookhouse. "I'm starved. Someone's sure fixing something good."

"I was going to take you to the ranger house," Pete said, "but maybe you'd all like to eat first. Charlie's got dinner just about ready."

After putting our saddlebags in a pile, we took our horses and mule back to the barn. I tied Red to a hitch rail, fed him oats, unsaddled him, and put his saddle and bridle in the shed next to the barn. His sweaty blanket lay on top of his saddle to dry. I brushed his back, chest, belly, and legs while he ate. Then I turned him out into the grassy area next to the corral. About 15 horses and mules waited to greet the new arrivals.

Red took a long drink from a water tank before moving among the other animals. His back, still wet from sweat, showed the outline of his saddle. He buckled his knees to the ground and rolled in the dusty dirt, waving his hooves in the air. It has always amazed me that such huge creatures can roll so easily onto their backs. I watched Rocky, Dillon, Smurf, and Kitty do the same.

The other horses and mules moved in among our animals, nickering a greeting. One horse nipped at a mule, sending it braying. One mule laid its ears flat on its head and kicked at another, moving it out of the way. Our animals held their own as the pecking order established itself. In the end, little Smurf ended up among the dominant ones. I wasn't surprised. He always had.

We walked back to the cookhouse. Everyone but Oriole and I went inside. I fed Oriole just outside the door and sat on a bench watching her wolf her food down before she fell into a deep sleep. It felt good to sit and rub my sore leg muscles.

Charlie Horton, the station guard, clanged a triangle bell by the door, right near where Oriole slept. I grimaced.

"Sorry it's so loud, but that's how we announce dinner," Charlie said softly.

Oriole opened her eyes, groaned, and went back to sleep.

"Come on in to dinner. Let's let sleeping dogs lie."

The Ghost of Schafer Meadows

Jed sat with his plate in his hands, staring at the food on the table with a giant grin on his face.

"I already love this place. Who fixed dinner?"

Pot roast with potatoes, onions, and carrots, salad with my favorite Ranch dressing, fresh hot homemade bread, cherry Kool-Aid, and hot apple pie filled the long table. We all sat together and ate family style.

"You can thank Charlie," Pete said. "He worked most of the day getting things ready. Wanted you to have a good hot meal after your long ride in."

As station guard, Charlie pretty much kept the Schafer Meadows Ranger Station running. Right away I thought he was really cool. Tall and white-haired with a white moustache, he wore western clothes and a bandana instead of a Forest Service uniform. He placed a small wooden bird on the table.

"Did you whittle that?" I asked.

Charlie's eyes twinkled and his moustache turned up slightly as he spoke softly. "I'm still working on it. But see the other carved wooden people and animals in the windowsill? Those are finished products."

"They look real," Mom said, picking one up.

"Well, thanks. They're something I like to do to keep me out of trouble." He stabbed a piece of pot roast as it went around the table. "So what are you going to do this summer, Jessie? Ride that horse of yours and rope bears?"

"Nah, bears are too easy. Thought I'd rope me a moose instead. They're meaner."

"You know, one of the early rangers tried that here once. Nearly got killed doing it."

"Yeah, right," I said, laughing.

"No, really. Look at the picture hanging on the wall over there."

Sure enough. There was a photo of a guy striking at a moose with a coiled horse bridle while the moose reared up on its hind legs and tried to thump the guy with its front hooves. My mouth hung open.

Charlie laughed softly. "I'm pulling your leg, Jessie. But what really happened is almost as unbelievable. A dog spooked the moose, who charged the man. The guy struck back with the bridle in self-defense. He sure was lucky. He ended up with some bad injuries requiring surgery, but he lived."

"What? You kidding me again?"

"Nope. Moose don't normally act like that, but look out when they do. They can be deadly."

Mandy Lake, Celie's other trail crew member, stared at the photo before turning back to her dinner. Mandy loosely gathered her bushy light brown hair with a band to keep it off her face. She had an easy smile and manner.

"What do you do for fun when you're not off working on some trail?" I asked Mandy.

"I like to spend time at the barn with the animals, grooming the horses and mules or just talking to them."

That instantly put her at the top of my list. I knew she'd get along great with Oriole.

"There are also incredible places to hike or backpack. You'll have to come along sometime, Jessie. Oriole can come, too. There are miles of places to explore."

After dinner we carried our own dishes to the counter, washed them in the sink, and put them in the dish rack. With everyone pitching in they went fast. Then Dad sat at the table, reading an old copy of the *Daily InterLake*, the Kalispell newspaper. It had come in with the last pack string.

"Listen to this," he said, reading from the front page. "Someone robbed a jewelry store in the Kalispell Center Mall, right in the middle of the day. The store had a big sale going on, with a huge inventory and a lot of really expensive pieces. Three thieves took cut diamonds, rubies, and other small gems from the store—no jewelry—but they stole about $100,000 worth."

Packer Brad let out a low whistle. "Wonder how they got away."

Dad continued reading. "It says there were a lot of people in the store for the sale, and three men surprised the owner at the back of the store, away from the customers. The owner wasn't hurt, but he never saw the men's faces—he just heard their voices.

"Also, an outfit was selling horse trailers in the parking lot and other stores had sales that had drawn a lot of people. The thieves just slipped out and blended in with the crowd. The police have no idea where the crooks went or how they escaped after the robbery."

"You know," Mom said, "when we first got to Spotted Bear, the Sheriff's Office was trying to radio all those deputies in the wilderness."

"Yeah, and Dad's boss Rosie said she was busy with some law enforcement stuff the day she gave us a tour," added Jed. "I bet it was related to that."

"Well," Dad said, "by now the thieves have probably been caught."

"I don't think so," Pete said. "We listen to local radio here in the cookhouse, one of the few places where we can usually get good reception, and so far we haven't heard anything on the news. We'll have to keep our ears tuned. Something this big doesn't happen very often around Kalispell."

As he sat at the table playing solitaire, his muscles bulging, Packer Brad grinned mischievously in my direction. "Have you ever seen a ghost?"

"Only the one of my brother in his pajamas on the way to the bathroom in the middle of the night," I said. "Talk about scary."

"Schafer has its own ghost, you know, and it hangs out a lot at the ranger's house."

Pulling her hair away from her face and tucking loose ends into her hair band, Mandy dismissed Packer Brad with a wave of her hand. "Oh give me a break. There's no ghost here. Don't listen to him, Jessie."

Packer Brad flipped over three cards and set them in a pile. "There is too a ghost. I've been here three years now and every year someone sees it."

"Oh, yeah, what does it look like?"

"I've heard it's a man who appears to people at night and sometimes calls out. I've also heard it's a woman who walks at night carrying a candle. But don't ask me. Ask someone who's seen the ghost." Packer Brad picked up a two of clubs and set it on a three of diamonds. "Like Pete."

My jaw dropped. "Did you really see the ghost, Pete?" As Oriole's rescuer and my friend, I trusted Pete to tell the truth, and it was hard to imagine that he would believe such a fantasy.

Pete, drinking coffee at the table, shifted uneasily in his chair. He pushed his mug away and sat still for a second. Then he shrugged his shoulders.

"First, let me say that normally I wouldn't believe in such a thing. But yep—I've seen the ghost. At least that's what it appeared to be."

"This is too cool!" Jed said, leaning over so he could see Pete, who sat two seats away on the same side of the table. "What happened?"

Pete was silent again. Then he said, "Which time?"

"WHICH TIME?" Mom, Dad, and Cody shouted in unison. He had everybody's attention now.

"Well, the first time I only heard him. The second time I saw him."

Pete walked to the coffee pot, poured himself another cup, and sat back down at the table, scraping his chair on the wood floor as he pulled it in with one hand. He took a sip of coffee, wrapping his large hands around the mug.

"Guess I'd better start at the beginning. The first time— the time I only heard him—was late one fall. Packer Brad was bringing mules into Schafer that day so he and I could close the station at the end of the season. The trail crew had already left. I was here alone. I had already turned off the water in all the buildings except here in the cookhouse, so I slept upstairs in the large storage room next to Charlie's room. It has a bed in there for people who need a place to stay when the bunkhouse is full." Pete waved toward the area at the back of the upstairs.

"Anyway, it was early in the morning, still dark. I heard a man call out, 'Hel-lo, Hel-lo.' I got up and went downstairs to the door. It had snowed during the night, enough that there would have been tracks if anyone had walked or ridden their horse past the cookhouse. But there were no tracks—none.

"I couldn't explain it," Pete said, confusion showing on his face. "That voice sounded so clear. I was sure someone was there."

"That doesn't prove there's a ghost," Packer Brad said. "You could have been dreaming."

Pete took another sip of coffee. "True, but my next encounter is harder to explain."

"So tell us," Mom said, clearly intrigued.

Pete took a deep breath and blew it out. "Last year we didn't have anyone in Tom's position as ranger, so I pretty much ran the station. I lived in the ranger's house. We had a big trail program, so two crew leaders lived in the house with me—in your room, Jed. Sometimes they'd go to the bunkhouse or cookhouse to play cards or games or just sit around and talk until late, so I was used to people wandering in and out of the house at all hours.

"One night I was asleep in bed. I woke up hearing the screen door squeak open and then bang shut. I heard soft footsteps come up the stairs. I didn't think much of it, because there's only the one bathroom, which we all shared.

"But the footsteps kept coming, past the bathroom and right into my room. Next thing I knew, I felt someone sit down at the foot of the bed. I could actually feel the bed sink down. Then I felt someone pressing down on the mattress on either side of my shoulders. I opened my eyes and saw the face of a man—a stranger—looking me right in the face. I could feel his ice-cold breath on my cheek."

Celie grabbed her braid and pulled it tightly over one shoulder with both hands. "Holy smoke! I'd have screamed my lungs out and run all the way back to Spotted Bear."

"Funny thing is I wasn't afraid. All I thought was, 'Oh. That's the ghost.' I rolled over, closed my eyes, and went back to sleep. I never even knew when he left."

Pete swallowed the rest of his coffee and set the mug gently on the table. "I'm not saying for sure it was the ghost. I've never been a believer. But I sure never experienced anything like that before—or since. Who knows? You may never see or hear the ghost the entire time you're here. Most people don't, right, Charlie?"

Charlie nodded, his red bandana nodding with him. "Right. I've been here for years and have only heard the stories. Never seen a thing."

Pete's story gave me the willies, but Charlie made me feel better. If he hadn't seen a ghost in all the years he worked at Schafer, maybe we wouldn't either.

No one could top Pete's tale, so we all just started leaving the table. It was time to see our new house.

Ghost or no ghost.

FIVE

The Ranger's House

"C'mon, I'll take you to the ranger's house, your new home," said Pete, hoisting a duffle bag under one arm and two of our sleeping bags under the other. "We've already got a lot of your gear there. Celie and Cody will bring the rest."

We ducked under the hitch rail and followed Pete to a log cabin near the cookhouse. Nestled in the pines by the edge of the airstrip, the two-story house had a porch with a big wooden swing. It looked like a cozy old cabin, not one haunted by a ghost.

Pete led us into the house through a squeaky screen door. A long couch and a couple of easy chairs took up most of the living room. Large windows faced the porch, airstrip, and cookhouse. The smell of wood smoke filled the air. A fire in the wood stove by the far wall crackled and warmed the room. An old wooden box next to the stove held stacked split wood.

Mom pointed to a spot just below the ceiling. "Good. There are propane gas lights on the walls. When you don't have electricity, it's nice not to have to light lanterns all the time."

"I know," said Pete. "We're lucky to have gas here at all. We can't have natural gas, it's too far to put in gas lines, but propane is just as good. The mules bring in propane tanks when we need them. They're nearly as tall as you, Jessie." He walked to a table that had a lantern on it. "There are lanterns if you want extra light, but the wall lights are usually all you'll need."

"What's in that room?" I asked, looking at a door just past the end of the couch.

"That's my bedroom," Jed said. "If it's okay with you, that is. I kinda moved in when Dad and I got here last week."

"Where am I gonna sleep?"

"Upstairs. You'll see."

We backed out of Jed's room and looked into the kitchen at the back of the house.

A small wooden table with four chairs hugged the wall next to the back door. A large sink, cupboards, and drawers under the counter filled another wall. Dad opened the cupboards and drawers to show us a few dishes, silverware, and glasses.

I looked around, more than a little worried. "Where's our refrigerator? Where's our food?"

"We won't eat meals here," Dad said. "We'll eat with everyone at the cookhouse."

"Good. At least that way we'll have lots of people to talk to so it won't be so lonely." I didn't care that my words stung Dad. I was still sore at him for making us move.

Pete pointed to a beautiful white antique wood-burning cook stove with silvery fixtures that faced into the kitchen with its back to Jed's room.

"That stove's been here a long time. They don't make them like that anymore."

Dad turned his sad-looking eyes from me to the antique cook stove. "So Pete, why's the cook stove here if not for cooking?"

"It's mostly kept here for backup heat if it really gets cold. Which isn't often. It's also a nice conversation piece, don't you think?"

"Can we see the upstairs?" I asked.

"Sure, let's go." Pete led the way.

The stairs to the second floor were against the living room wall on the side by the cookhouse. At the top right was a small bathroom with a sink, toilet, and an old-fashioned claw-foot bathtub. A shower curtain circled the tub on a suspended pole.

Pete pointed to a small white tank hanging on a wall above the sink. "This little guy heats up water on demand so you can have showers. The minute you turn on the water it's hot."

"That's great," Mom said. "I wasn't sure how we would get hot water to bathe. I had visions of us heating buckets of water."

We continued down the short hallway. It ended at a bedroom with a queen-sized bed. "This is our bedroom," Dad said to Mom, "complete with a dresser and closet. Pretty cushy compared to what we had in the wilderness in New Mexico, isn't it? And the window faces the airstrip, so we can hear the horses and mules at night as they graze on the strip."

"Oh, wonderful, Tom," Mom said sarcastically. "I hope I get some sleep."

Dad put his arm around her. "Don't worry, Kate. The horses and mules usually hang out at one end of the airstrip or the other. I haven't heard them at night except occasionally when they gallop by or one of them snorts or bellows. Mostly I hear the bell one of them wears. To me it's comforting knowing they're still around and haven't run off."

"So this is where Pete met the ghost face-to-face," I said looking around the room. "Scare ya much, Dad?"

"No, Jessie. If the ghost didn't hurt Pete, I don't think it will bother us. Besides, your mother's pretty tough. She'll keep me safe."

Mom shook a finger at Dad. "If those horses and mules aren't quiet at night I might just call on that ghost to help me run them off for good."

Jed looked out the window. "Holy smoke! Look there."

"The ghost?" I asked.

Everyone crowded to the window. A mother moose and her new baby ambled across the airstrip. I'd never seen a moose except on TV. The newborn had long wobbly legs and kept close to its mother's side. The mother nudged her tiny baby with her long nose.

"I thought moose had antlers," I said. "How come this one doesn't?"

"Only males have them," Pete said.

Mom stood on her tiptoes looking over Jed's shoulder, watching the two animals. "Aren't they beautiful! Maybe living next to the airstrip won't be so bad after all."

We watched until they went into the woods before we left the room.

"Okay," I said, fighting back a sudden panic. "Where's my bedroom? There's no other room up here." I glared at Jed. "Pretty funny, Jed. Do I have to sleep on the floor in Mom and Dad's room or were you thinking I'd sleep in your bedroom with you?"

"Neither," Dad said, sharing a secret wink with Jed. "Look here."

He pointed to a door at the top of the stairs opposite the bathroom. The roof sloped down to the outer wall. "This space was used for storage in the past, but Jed and I worked all last week to turn it into a loft-like bedroom. It's small, but if you like it, it's yours."

I walked in. The room held a bed and a dresser for my clothes and still had plenty of space for Oriole's pad. I liked it—a lot.

Able to breathe again, I said, "I always dreamed of living in a loft in the mountains. This is the next best thing. Thanks for fixing this for me, you guys. Sorry I got mad, Jed. You're the greatest!" I mentally started to move in, but then another moment of panic hit me. "Where's Oriole?"

We all looked around. She wasn't there.

We went downstairs. The screen door was ajar. I thought she might have let herself out and gone exploring, but Pete relieved my fears once more. "Look over there," he said, pointing to a rug in front of the couch.

Curled up, nose to tail, lay Oriole. She was sound asleep. "Our 20-mile trip in here was about 40 miles for Oriole with all the running back and forth that she did," whispered Dad as he scooped her up in his arms. "No wonder she's pooped."

Dad carried her upstairs and put her on my bed. I ran my hand along Oriole's black eye and ear. "I hope she wakes up if the ghost comes."

"Don't worry too much about the ghost, Jessie. We've all had a long day. Why don't you go to bed and try to sleep."

Exhausted, I said good night, put on my pajamas, and crawled in next to Oriole. I don't even remember my head hitting the pillow.

That night I saw a man standing at the foot of my bed staring at me. He wore an old felt cowboy hat and torn clothing. A stubbly beard made soft scratching noises when his head moved across his shirt. I tried to ask him what he wanted, but words wouldn't come out of my mouth. He watched me through sad-looking eyes for a while before turning away and walking down the stairs. Was it a dream? I didn't know. I only knew I wasn't afraid. He didn't seem to want to harm me.

The Pilot

The next morning I thought about the ghost as Oriole and I watched Packer Brad and his mule string leave from the barn for the long trail back to Spotted Bear. I still wasn't scared and soon forgot about it.

Oriole and I tagged along with Cody and Mandy to the bunkhouse, a long one-story log building close to the cookhouse. It had one room with about half a dozen single metal beds and another room with a bathroom and shower. I thought people would feel cramped in there, but Mandy reminded me that the crew didn't sleep there very often. Mostly they stayed in tents or backcountry cabins near the trail they were working on and only came back to Schafer on their days off. Even then they'd often go backpacking or hike out to somewhere else. So the bunkhouse was usually empty.

Mom was busy setting up her "office" when Oriole and I got back to the house. Years ago Mom taught college history, but when Dad's work took us from one place to another, it was too hard for her to keep a job. She always wanted to be a writer, so one day she began writing romance novels set in some historical time period, like the Civil War or when settlers moved west.

It's funny. I always thought someone who wrote love stories would wear pearls and high heels. Instead, Mom usually sits at the computer dressed in jeans and a T-shirt, her shoulder-length blonde hair in a ponytail sticking out from under a baseball cap, her tall thin body sitting ramrod straight.

As she thinks up stories, her blue eyes get a distant look and her fingers fly across the keyboard. She's good at what she writes—good enough that we can live anywhere that Dad's job takes us. If Mom keeps cranking out novels, maybe someday we won't have to move again.

She put her laptop on a small wooden table in the living room next to the front window. Because Schafer had no electricity, Mom needed a constant supply of computer batteries. And she couldn't use a printer. How primitive can you get? All her work had to be put on a CD to mail out. She stored stacks of CDs and about ten backup batteries in a cardboard box below the table.

"What are you and Oriole up to today?" Mom asked.

"I thought I might work on some more obedience lessons with her and then take Red for a ride."

"Well, don't go too far with Red until you know the area better."

"I won't. I might take him out on the airstrip and run him a bit to give him some exercise."

"Okay. Enjoy yourself, but be careful. See you at lunch." Mom sat down to work on her book.

Oriole and I dashed to the airstrip. I taught her to come, sit, stay, and lie down following only hand signals. She already knew voice commands, but I figured sometime she might be too far away to hear me or I might not want to speak. Knowing hand signals might save her life.

The morning was sunny and getting warmer by the minute. I rewarded Oriole for being a good student with a swim in the river. We found a deep hole where the water didn't flow too fast, and she swam for a long time. The water seemed to invigorate her and when we left the river she raced up to the cookhouse, leaving wet footprints and a trail of water in the dirt.

We stopped in for a bowl of water for Oriole and a glass of lemonade for me. Charlie was in his little office in the back

room of the kitchen. I could hear him talking on the radio to
Spotted Bear. Through the static, Cindy, the woman from the
front desk at Spotted Bear, relayed to him that his friend from
Kalispell was flying into Schafer that afternoon to visit. Oriole
lay down by the table while I drank my lemonade.

"Does your friend have his own plane?" I asked Charlie
when he came out.

"He does. He likes to come to Schafer, mostly to give me
a hard time and make my life miserable," Charlie joked. "He's
coming for a couple of days to fish and camp."

"Great. Maybe at least he likes kids and dogs."

"Nope. He eats 'em for lunch, so you better be scarce
while he's around."

I finished my lemonade. Charlie started sweeping the
floor. Seemed like a good time for Oriole and me to split.

Dad and Jed were at the house when we got back. Mom
sat at her laptop, so intent on her book that she didn't seem
to know we were there. Jed was stuffing work gloves into his
saddlebags.

"What's up?" I asked.

"Jed's going with Pete to pack Celie, Cody, and Mandy
into a trail camp tomorrow," Dad said. "They'll drop them off
and then bring the horses and mules back."

"Wow, can I go, too?"

"Not this time. Opening a trail for the first time in the
season can be tough, especially if a lot of trees fall across it
during the winter."

"I know, but I can help get the trees off the trail."

"No, Jessie. It's hard work and sometimes takes hours to
clear a trail. It may be a long time before the crew gets into
camp. You can go along with me later when there won't be
those kinds of problems to worry about."

"You make me feel like a little kid. I can carry logs and
help just as much as anyone else."

"Soon, honey, I promise," Dad said, walking to the stairs. "But this time you can stay here and keep Mom company and help Charlie if you want."

I opened the squeaky screen door and slammed it behind me. "Some summer this is going to be," I grumbled, loud enough so I hoped Dad would hear. "I want to go home to New Mexico."

I sat on the swing with my arms folded over my chest, hoping Dad would come out and say he'd changed his mind. I sat for a long time. Finally I opened the door and called Oriole. She bounded out and wagged her tail, grabbing a stick and tossing it into the air. I ignored her, muttering to myself all the way to the barn.

Red stood just outside the corral, close enough to catch easily. I brushed him, my hurt feelings coming out with every stroke. Meanwhile Oriole barked a challenge to a squirrel, who chattered its response from the safety of a tree limb. Oriole was having a great time. She didn't seem to care that I was mad.

After saddling Red, I got on and walked him around a bit, doing some circle eights before we began to trot the length of the airstrip. Until then I didn't realize how long the airstrip was. It must have been a half mile of short-cropped grass. The horses and mules had lots to eat when they grazed on the airstrip at night.

Oriole stayed either next to Red or just behind him. When her red tongue hung out of her mouth and her breath came hard and fast, I made her lie down under a tree to rest.

By then I had calmed down somewhat, thinking that maybe it wouldn't be so bad to have someone do all the hard work before I helped with the trail projects. I thought of myself as a princess with all of my servants going before me, clearing the way, carrying all of my worldly goods so I didn't have to do anything but ride Red. I would thank my servants when we arrived at our destination, giving them extra rations at the end of the day for their hard work.

The morning slipped away. By the time I walked Red back, Oriole was lying by the gate to the airstrip. She got up and greeted us, yawning and stretching. Hearing the drone of a plane overhead, I quickly took Red to the corral, unsaddled and brushed him, and turned him loose. Red drank water from the trough as Oriole and I ran back to the airstrip.

A small white plane buzzed the airstrip and circled back, its engine slowing as the pilot touched down. The plane turned around at the end of the runway. The engine's deafening roar reverberated against the mountains as the pilot taxied to the other end of the airstrip. A short stocky man about Charlie's age got out.

Oriole and I ran to meet him. I was about to say something when Oriole began to growl, backing away.

The man's lip curled. "Hey, kid! Get that dog away from me!"

Oriole began to bark loudly, the hackles standing up on her back. "Oriole, what's wrong with you?" I grabbed her by the collar. "I'm sorry, mister. She's never done this before to anyone. Charlie'll be mad at me when he finds out Oriole treated his friend so badly."

"Who's Charlie?" The man stared at Oriole, keeping his distance from her.

"Aren't you Charlie's friend?"

"Never heard of him, kid. Just take me to whoever's in charge." He walked past me like I didn't exist. So much for being a princess. I was now this guy's slave.

Oriole had stopped barking, so I let go of her collar. She walked along next to me, occasionally giving a low growl in the man's direction. She really didn't seem to like him and let him know it.

We walked to the cookhouse in silence. I took the man inside and left him with Charlie while I went to find Dad. I heard Charlie offering him something to drink.

Oriole's reaction to the man made me wonder about her life before she came to live with us.

I found Dad at the house. "Hey, Dad, do you know if Oriole was abused before you got her at the animal shelter? There's a guy who just flew in and Oriole didn't like him one bit. She really growled and barked at him. I thought she might go after him for a minute."

"I never heard anything about that. She was just a puppy, but that doesn't mean she wasn't abused. Did the guy do anything to Oriole—you know—strike at her, raise his hand like he would, try to scare her away?"

"No, he was just really unpleasant. And guess what? It's your lucky day. He wants to see you."

Dad sighed. "I hate this part of my job. Why do some people come all this way carrying a chip on their shoulder? Most visitors want to be here. Oh, well. Better go see what he wants."

Oriole and I followed Dad to the cookhouse. The man sat at the table, drinking coffee and chowing down on Cody's homemade chocolate chip cookies like they were going out of style. Cody had won awards for those cookies, and I despised seeing that man eat even one of them. At the rate he was going, there wouldn't be any left for the rest of us. Oriole lay on the floor near Charlie, staring at the man.

Charlie leaned against the stairs, eyes on the man as he said to Dad, "Tom, this is Hank Cooter. He's from Kalispell and just came to check the place out. Says he's got some friends who might come in on horseback some day soon."

"You in charge?" Cooter said, looking at Dad through cold watery eyes.

Dad stepped forward and stuck out his hand. "I'm Tom Scott, the ranger here."

Cooter ignored Dad's hand, choosing instead to stuff another of my beloved cookies in his mouth. Dad stood with his arms crossed, his lips a thin line. I thought he was going to blow up at the guy, but instead, he took a deep breath and said, "What can we do for you, Hank?"

"Nothing, really. Just wanted to see how you government bureaucrats work back here." He sniggered. "Got it pretty soft here, don't you?"

Dad's face got red but he stayed cool. "Look, we've got a lot of work to do. Our crew is leaving tomorrow to open trails, and we're trying to get the station ready for summer visitors. Now if you want or need something, let me know. Otherwise go to the campground or wherever you intend to go and we'll go back to doing our jobs."

Dad took the plate of cookies away and put it on the counter. *Way to go, Dad!*

Cooter stood up. "Man can't even get a cup of coffee and a cookie without someone giving him grief. No need to be unfriendly. I was just leaving."

By this time Oriole was standing and growling again. "Better watch that mangy fur ball. That's one vicious dog." He set his cup down on the table, hitched up his pants, and swaggered to the door. "You government types are all the same," he said loudly as the door slammed behind him. "Ought to write my congressman."

Charlie and Dad just looked at each other, shaking their heads. Charlie took the empty coffee cup from the table, carried it by one finger through the handle hole like it had some kind of disease, and put it in the sink. He washed his hands well before he picked up a small square piece of wood and began whittling. "It's a good thing people like him don't come back here often. They sure can make your job hard."

"We'd better keep an eye on him," Dad said. "I don't know what he's up to, but I doubt we've heard the last from Hank Cooter." He turned to me. "You make sure Oriole stays far away from him, Jessie. She's obviously got good taste in people because she doesn't like him at all, but she could get into real trouble. We know she doesn't have a mean bone in her body, but I don't want to give Cooter any ammunition to harm her."

"Okay, Dad. I'll be real careful." I hugged Oriole to me, fearful of something awful happening to her.

Just then another plane buzzed the airstrip. Looking out the door, Charlie folded and pocketed his knife and set down his new carving. "There's Jim. Let's go get him. He'll brighten our day."

A small plane, blue on top and white below, landed and taxied back toward the station. The door opened and a tall man about Charlie's age, wearing a blue baseball cap with an airplane on it, jumped out. He immediately bent over and started wrestling with Oriole. She ran around him, barking happily. The man dropped to his knees to pat her, and she licked his face. *She's not afraid of this person*, I thought.

"We were wrong about that dog of yours, Jessie," Charlie said, as we reached the man. "She doesn't have very good taste in people after all."

"Horton, you old goat," the man said, pumping Charlie's hand and slapping him on the back. "Stop telling lies. How do you ever expect me to meet beautiful women like this one here if you keep scaring them away?"

Charlie chuckled. "This is Jim Gunderson from Bigfork, just outside Kalispell. We worked together years ago. This is Tom and Jessie Scott and Oriole."

Jim shook our hands and scratched Oriole on the head before walking back to his plane. He stuck his hand behind the pilot's seat, brought out a small cooler with a paper bag on top, and carried them back to us. "Charlie told me there was a special person and her dog here that I needed to meet. I brought something for both of you."

He sat the cooler on the ground and opened it. It contained a gallon tub of vanilla ice cream. Holding the bag just out of reach of Oriole's nose he said, "This one's for your dog. It's dog biscuits. Figured I'd better make friends with the important people here first. That way maybe I'll be allowed to stay."

"You can stay as long as you want," I said, staring at the cooler like Oriole stared at the bag. "Anyone who brings ice cream is a friend of mine. And you sure made points with Oriole."

Jim carried the cooler to the cookhouse. Charlie took the ice cream from Jim and put it in the basement freezer. I gave Oriole a biscuit and closed the bag. The rest would go to the house for her to eat later.

"Who has the other plane?" Jim asked as he sat and drank some grape Kool-Aid.

"Guy named Hank Cooter from Kalispell. Know him?" Dad asked.

"Can't say that I do."

"He's the kind that gives pilots a bad name," said Charlie. "Real unfriendly sort. Didn't offer a lot of information and he didn't seem to want anything from us."

"Is he staying long?"

"Don't know. He said he's staying in the campground tonight. That's all I got out of him before Tom and Jessie came in. I'd be careful around him, Jim. He's got a real mean streak."

"Swell. But changing the subject, I called Spotted Bear to see if they needed anything brought in. They told me the trail crew is going out tomorrow, so I brought enough steaks, spuds, and baked beans for everyone. Thought we could have a barbeque tonight at my campsite. That way I know I'll get something good to eat. I don't ever try to rely on Charlie's cooking."

"Well, it's about time you stopped mooching off me," Charlie said.

"Think I should invite Cooter?" asked Jim. "We might learn some more about him if we do."

"It's up to you," Dad said. "It might be pretty unpleasant having him around, but if you don't invite him and he's the only other person at the campground, it might make things even worse."

"I'll ask him. If he's as bad as you say, my guess is he won't come. But at least we'll have made an effort and he can't complain." Jim put his glass in the sink. "Think I'll go to the campground and set up my tent. Then I want to see if Charlie left any fish in the river."

"Can Oriole and I come with you?" I asked.

"Sure, bring your pole. Meet me after lunch and we'll see if we can't scare up some fish to have with our steak for dinner."

SEVEN

The Light

I made sure I had a couple of Cody's chocolate chip cookies for lunch, just in case that old coot Hank came back again. After lunch I grabbed my fishing gear and whistled to Oriole. We met Jim in the campground sitting at a picnic table close to the airstrip. He had already put up his tall green dome tent.

Jim grabbed his rod and tackle box. "Ready to show those fish who's boss?"

"I'm not very good at catching fish, but I sure like to chase them around."

"Well, I'm not the best, but maybe I can give you some pointers."

We spent the afternoon walking up and down along the river, fishing in places Jim thought would be good. We could see into some deep holes. Green, gray, and red rocks covered the river bottom. In some places tree roots snaked their way underwater, reaching for the bottom like long gnarled fingers. A few trout hid in the deepest pools under the shade of the trees, ignoring our lures. A light breeze rustled the cottonwood trees, and birds chirped and flitted from branch to branch in the shrubby willows. We kept moving, casting out our lures and watching them drift by. Sometimes rushing waters rolled over boulders, creating small rapids that roared past us.

Oriole amused herself by chasing sticks along the bank and swimming when the river was calm enough. She took a long nap in the warm sun when we stopped for a break, occasionally whimpering in her sleep while her legs moved and her nose twitched. Jim and I laughed, trying to guess what she was dreaming.

"I bet she's chasing rabbits," he said quietly.

"I bet she's chasing Hank Cooter," I whispered, looking around first to make sure he wasn't within earshot. I had told Jim how badly Hank had treated Oriole.

"Well, I want you to know I think she's a great dog and you've done a tremendous job training her. For as young as she is she's extremely well behaved. You two are very lucky to have each other and to live out here. This is one of my favorite places in the world."

I felt like I could confide in Jim. "I'm still kind of mad at Dad for taking me away from New Mexico and my friends. He has no idea how hard it was on me."

"I bet he does, Jessie. Don't forget, your dad had to leave his friends and home just like you. He's probably having a hard time, too."

I never thought about that before. "Maybe so. But I haven't told him yet that I really kinda like it here. Everyone so far except that crude dude Hank has been super, and Oriole keeps me busy. Maybe Schafer will become one of my favorite places, too. I'm—oh wow! I caught another one!"

Jim helped me get the fish into the net. "That makes just about enough for dinner. What do you say we call it a day and head back? Charlie'll give me a hard time if I don't have everything perfect for dinner by the time everyone gets there."

"Can I ask you a question first, Jim?"

"Fire away."

"You've spent a lot of time back here visiting Charlie. Did you ever see a ghost or hear stories of one? People sure have been talking a lot about that, but I don't know."

"I've heard stories on occasion."

"Do you believe them? I don't—at least I haven't—but I'm a little scared. Last night I thought a man was in my room.

Do you think it could be the ghost?"

"I don't know what to tell you, but I've never heard anyone at Schafer say a ghost harmed them."

"I just wonder who it might be."

"I wouldn't know. Maybe Charlie or someone who's been here a while could give you their thoughts."

We retrieved the fish string from the water and walked back to Jim's campsite.

"Why don't you go home, Jessie? I can clean the fish myself."

"Are you sure? I don't mind helping." I really did—cleaning fish was pretty gross if you asked me—but I owed it to him after taking me with him all afternoon.

"Thanks, but I've got dinner pretty well under control. It was fun, though. We'll have to do it again."

We went to Jim's campsite at 6 p.m. Celie had made Indian tacos with fry bread, a Blackfeet tradition, and Mandy contributed a huge salad. Cody baked a chocolate cake to go along with the ice cream, which Pete carried in a cooler. We were set.

Jim had steaks and fish sizzling on the grill when we arrived, and he cooked them to order. I'd never tasted better, maybe because Jim grilled over mesquite wood chips he had brought in on the plane. Or maybe because Hank Cooter chose not to join us for dinner and I knew I didn't have to be around him. He had pitched his tent on the other side of the campground and sat with his back to us the whole time we ate. That was fine with me and everyone else.

We all laughed and talked and listened to stories from Charlie and Jim about the old days in the backcountry. The crew was eager to get started on their trail project in the morning, so they talked about their gear, making sure they had what they would need for the next ten days. Jim gathered firewood and we made a campfire. I sat on a camp chair I had brought from the house.

"Look there." Jim pointed to the airstrip.

The mother moose and her baby ambled past. We watched them feed on grass uphill and upwind from us.

A clear evening slowly turned into a black night. Stars filled the sky, twinkling and glittering.

"There's the North Star," I said. "It's my favorite because no matter where I am it gives me a sense of direction."

The North Star came out with the Big Dipper. The Milky Way spread out over our heads like a speckled road in the sky.

"I've always loved looking at stars and finding the constellations," Jim said. "And being a pilot I've wanted to learn to navigate by them."

The campground had an outhouse, close to Hank Cooter's campsite. When I couldn't wait any longer, I walked quickly and quietly to the outhouse, hoping Hank wouldn't hear me and turn around. But he wasn't sitting at his table anymore. A light lit up the inside of his tent. He must have gone there to sulk.

Back at Jim's campsite, Celie was telling Native American stories about the stars. It seemed everyone had some kind of tale to tell about the night sky.

About 10:30 I got tired and decided to go home to bed. I walked over to Mom and Dad and told them I was going back to the house.

"Good night, everyone," I said. "Thanks for a great dinner and a fun afternoon, Jim. We'll have to show Charlie how to catch fish sometime."

"You're on," Charlie said. "Soon."

"Come on, Oriole. Let's go to bed."

I had my flashlight, but the bright starlight allowed me to see the dark shape of the barn and then the cookhouse, so I left it off. I had just reached the far side of the bunkhouse when I saw a light shining in the living room of our house. Mom and Dad hadn't turned on any lights before we left for dinner, so what was that all about?

Fear took hold of me as I watched the light move. Could it be the ghost? I froze in my tracks. It had to be!

Softly, I said, "Oriole! Come quickly."

We hurried quietly to the side of the bunkhouse. Oriole sat while I leaned against the wall, peeking around the corner. The light moved again. It went from the living room into Jed's room. Then it seemed to float back into the living room and then into the kitchen. My heart pounded in my throat. I wanted to run but couldn't. All I could do was watch. My breath came in hard bursts.

The light was like some evil being, searching every corner of the kitchen. It turned in my direction, and I ducked back behind the bunkhouse wall so it couldn't see me.

"Whoa, that was close!" I gasped to Oriole. "We gotta be careful."

It roamed around in the kitchen for a long time, and I grew more and more frightened the longer we stayed in our hiding place.

Finally I couldn't stand it any more. Turning around and clicking on my flashlight, I whispered, "Oriole, let's go!"

We ran as quietly as possible back to the campground. Pete sat nearest the path. Out of breath, I called him aside.

"What's up, Jessie? You look like you've seen a ghost."

"I think I have. On our way to the house I saw a light moving around inside. Did you ever see the ghost do that?"

"No, Jessie, but I doubt that's what you saw. All those stories you heard about the ghost probably have your brain working overtime. C'mon. I'll walk over with you and we'll see if we can't figure this out ourselves."

"Oh, thanks, Pete! I don't want everyone to think I'm a chicken."

Pete, Oriole, and I headed back toward the house. When we reached the bunkhouse, I returned to the wall where I had watched the light. Once more I peeked around the corner. There were no lights. The house was dark.

"I know there was a light, Pete! I'm not imagining it. It moved all around downstairs and stayed for a long time."

"I'm sorry Jessie, but I sure don't see anything out of the ordinary. Let's go into the house and see if anything looks strange."

The screen door squeaked our arrival and I cringed, thinking any ghost would hear us. Pete entered first, striking a match to turn on a gas light by the woodstove so we could see. Everything looked just like we'd left it.

Then Oriole let out a low growl. Pete and I stood still and listened. We didn't hear anything.

"What's wrong, Oriole?" I asked quietly.

Oriole growled again and walked stealthily toward Jed's room. She held her head high and sniffed the air. Pete rested his hand on my arm to stop me from following him. "Stay here," he said quietly, both to me and Oriole.

Slowly, Pete walked toward Jed's room. He grabbed a poker from the woodstove as he went by. Cautiously he entered the room. I could see his back. He stood for a moment in the doorway. Then his shoulders relaxed and he dropped his arms, letting out a deep breath.

"Nothing here. I don't know what upset Oriole. Let's keep looking."

We walked back into the living room and then into the kitchen. Oriole growled again and raised her hackles.

"I don't get it. There's nothing here either," I said, "but something is really bugging Oriole. She hasn't growled in this house once since we got here. I thought the ghost was friendly, but she sure doesn't think so."

"There's nothing here to indicate that there's a ghost,"

Pete said, putting the poker back as he walked toward the door. "Or anything else for that matter. Is anything out of place?"

When I shook my head, he said, "We know that everyone who works here was at the barbeque tonight. And we know Hank Cooter was in the campground. No one saw him leave. Let's go back to the campground and get your folks. I think you'll feel better if they come back with you."

"Okay, but I'll feel pretty silly when they hear I saw a light and then it disappeared."

"I wouldn't worry about that. It's better to tell someone, just in case."

As Pete and I started back we saw Mom, Dad, and Jed coming our way. We waited for them on the porch.

"Mom, Dad, I've got something to tell you."

"What is it, Jessie?" Mom asked. "You look frightened."

We told them what had happened and they didn't laugh at me, even when I said I thought the ghost had visited the house. That made me feel better.

"No one who works here would enter the house without your permission," Pete said, "but did you happen to see Hank Cooter before you left?"

"Why, yes, I did," Mom said. "I saw him come out of his tent and head to the outhouse about the time we left. You saw him, didn't you, Tom?"

"No, Kate. I had my back to his tent. Guess that leaves him out as a suspect. We'll keep an eye out for anything suspicious. I don't think you saw a ghost, Jessie, so we'll just call it a mystery until we find something else."

Pete left to go to bed. My parents, Jed, and I sat and talked a bit more. Dad said there was probably nothing to worry about.

"Schafer is a very safe place, and there are lots of people around. But just to be cautious, I'll call Spotted Bear tomorrow and have them let the law enforcement people know what you saw, Jessie."

When we went to bed, I brought Oriole up and wrapped my arms around her. I felt safe having her sleeping with me, knowing her great hearing and excellent nose would alert us to any danger.

I fell asleep dreaming of ghosts.

EIGHT

Flying

"Come boys!" I awoke next morning to someone shouting outside the house and rattling a can. I ran to the window in Mom and Dad's room. The wranglers were on the airstrip, shaking a can of compressed alfalfa pellets the size of my thumb to entice the horses and mules to come to them. It was time to get the animals off the airstrip for the day.

"Come boys!" I watched a stampede of horses and mules thunder past our house on their way to the barn. They knew it was breakfast time.

The wranglers, who this time happened to be Mandy, Cody, and Jed, got the horses and mules fed and saddled so they'd be ready when the trail crew left for their work project. I didn't want anyone to leave. It would be a lot quieter at Schafer without them. It would also be way spookier with fewer people around if the ghost came back for another visit.

On my way to the cookhouse for breakfast, I heard a loud "vroom" as a plane engine came to life. Hank Cooter's plane began to move, first slowly and then faster and faster, lifting off the ground just before the end of the runway. *Goodbye and good riddance,* I thought.

In the cookhouse, the trail crew finished eating.

"Hey," I said. "Someone shouted 'Come boys!' this morning to the horses. Aren't there any mares?"

Cody took his plate to the sink to wash. "Not normally, Jessie. They'd distract the geldings—males—and there might be fights. It's too much trouble."

I bolted down my food so I could say goodbye to everyone. Mandy and Jed had tied the horses and mules to the hitch rail at the back of the cookhouse and were putting the manty packs on the mules. Mandy hoisted one heavy manty that must have weighed close to 100 pounds, set it against a mule's saddle, and wrapped a rope tightly around it, securing it to a ring on top of the saddle. Jed put another manty on the mule's other side. They loaded the manties so the weight on each side was even, making it easier and safer for the mule to carry its heavy cargo. The animal just stood there like it was no big deal, even closing its eyes as if ready for a nap.

Dad gave last minute instructions to the crew and told them he'd be out to visit soon. Celie, Cody, and Mandy looked like construction workers in hard hats, gloves, high-topped leather boots, long pants, and long-sleeved shirts. They hiked in the lead, carrying only their backpacks.

Jed rode behind them on Rocky, guiding the pack string, his cowboy hat shading his face. He held a rope in one hand that was attached to the first mule's halter. Another rope tied to a loop on the back of the mule's saddle was then secured to the next mule's halter and so on. All the animals were attached together. They walked single-file as they carried their heavy loads down the trail. Pete rode in the rear so he could watch the mules in case their packs slipped and needed an adjustment.

"See ya," I said to the crew, waving as they walked away.

"Be safe," Dad said, also waving. Then to me he said, "How'd you like to take a plane ride this morning with Jim?"

"Would I! I'd love to. Where are we going? How long will we be gone?"

"Whoa. Hold on a second," Dad said to stop me from asking any more questions. "Before he left Kalispell yesterday Jim found out he had some important business papers to sign. They weren't ready yet, but a friend of his plans to camp near Spotted Bear tonight and said he'd bring them today and meet

Jim at the Spotted Bear airstrip. Jim plans to make a short stop at the ranger station after that and return to Schafer this afternoon."

"That'd be incredible, Dad. I'll go talk to Jim now."

Dad smiled. "I think I heard him in the cookhouse talking with Charlie and your mother."

With Oriole at my heels, I burst through the cookhouse door, full of questions for Jim, but he caught me off guard.

"Would you like to take Oriole?"

"You're kidding!"

"No, I'm not. She'd have to ride in the back seat, and I'd want to circle the station a couple of times first just in case she gets scared and doesn't want to fly. If that happens, we can land again and let her out."

"When can we go?" I asked, practically dancing with joy.

"How soon can you be ready?"

"I'm ready!"

Jim asked me to pack us a lunch while he got the plane ready to go. Dad and Mom reminded me of the safety training I'd had about flying in the mountains. I had flown in small planes many times when we lived in New Mexico, but the Forest Service requires a review of all safety precautions before every trip. When Oriole and I got to the plane, Jim showed me the emergency beacon switch and survival gear, how to position my body in case we had "an unscheduled landing," how to speak to him through the microphone in my helmet, and lots of other safety messages about flying.

Mom handed me some CDs, an envelope to put them in, and postage. She also gave me an armload of rechargeable laptop batteries and asked me to exchange them for other batteries in our house at Spotted Bear.

Oriole jumped into the back seat. Dad and Mom gave me a hug and I swung into the front seat on the passenger's side. Then Jim got in and we were ready to go.

"Got your camera?" Jim asked. Mainly he wanted to know if I could hear him through my helmet and if I could push the button on my microphone to respond.

"Camera's ready. I can't wait to take some photos from the air. It'll be awesome."

"Well, let's get to it then," Jim said.

He started the engine. The plane came to life. I looked in the back seat. Oriole's eyes were huge.

Jim saw her, too. "I read that dogs hear far better than humans. The noise must be deafening for her."

"It's too bad there's not a headset for dogs to wear. Maybe that'll be my big invention."

Jim checked all the switches and gauges he needed to test before takeoff. Then he slowly taxied the plane. We bumped our way out onto the grassy runway. Jim stopped the plane and contacted Kalispell City Airport with a flight plan. A pilot always has a plan and someone knows where the plane is at all times and when it's expected to arrive at its destination.

We were ready to go. The engine got louder and louder, and the plane shook like it would lift off the ground before we even began to taxi. Oriole had moved. She had her back legs on the seat, her front paws on the floor, and her head on my arm. She didn't look too sure about flying.

We taxied down the runway, picking up speed, staying on the ground for what seemed like forever. Then suddenly we were airborne, and the plane climbed and climbed.

Jim looked straight ahead. "How's Oriole doing?"

She still sat in her takeoff position, her head reaching farther up my arm. She tried to get as close to me as possible. "I think she's okay, but let's do the two circles you suggested."

While Jim circled I talked to Oriole and stroked her head. "It's okay, Oriole. You know I wouldn't do anything to hurt you. Just take it easy."

Oriole sat stiffly for a while and then slowly began to relax. By the time we started into the second circle she looked like she thought maybe all would be okay. I gave Jim a *thumbs-up* and he banked the plane in the direction of Spotted Bear.

We flew above the same trail that our family had ridden into Schafer. Everywhere we looked we saw mountains, mountains, and more mountains. Even the biggest ones appeared tiny from the air. Snow still covered most of them. The highest ones were rocky and treeless on top. The lowest mountains had thick trees that blended together so it looked like a dark green sea. Some had trails that zigzagged up and up from far below before they disappeared into the snow.

I wondered if the crew would have to clear the trails of snow. That would be a lot of shoveling. I bet they probably just waited for it to melt.

The sun shone brightly on the mountains. The cloudless sky and crisp clean air brought everything into sharp focus. I snapped pictures left and right as we flew, hoping my new digital camera took good photos. I couldn't wait to send some to the Two J's in New Mexico to make them jealous of me.

Jim glanced into the backseat. "Looks like Oriole's a seasoned flyer now." I turned around to see her sitting on the seat behind me, staring out the window and wagging her tail.

I beamed. "Oriole's pretty amazing. I should have named her 'No Fear.' She may be afraid for a while but when she figures out that something's not dangerous she gets into it and has fun."

The flight was short. What took us most of a day on horseback took only about a half hour by plane. Before I knew it we were flying next to the South Fork River and then landing on Spotted Bear's grassy airstrip. Touching down didn't seem any more bumpy than if we'd been in a big plane at a large airport.

Jim got out of the plane and waved to a man standing next to a truck. He walked toward him.

"Hey, Jim, is it okay with you if Oriole and I join you in a couple of minutes?" I said. "I want to take a few pictures here."

"No problem. We'll wait for you 'til you're done."

Oriole and I walked toward the edge of the trees closest to the river. A horse trailer was parked nearby, and a small white plane was just down the runway from the trailer.

"Oriole, look how pretty the plane and trailer look against the mountains. This'd be a great picture to show the Two J's back home."

I snapped a couple of photos before a familiar but unwelcome form walked out of the woods towards us.

"Well, if it isn't Tweedle Dumb and Tweedle Dumber," said Hank Cooter.

NINE

Break-In at the Food Cache

Hank Cooter was the last person I wanted to see right then. Apparently Oriole felt the same way, because she began her low growl.

"Keep that mutt away from me," Hank snarled. He kicked out in her direction.

"Oh, don't worry. This dog has more sense than you do. She doesn't want to be anywhere near you. Why can't you come around us without saying something nasty?"

I was about to say more when I felt a firm hand land on my shoulder.

"Look, Hank," said Jim, who seemed to appear out of nowhere. "We didn't come here for a confrontation. Why don't you just mind your own business and be on your way."

Hank Cooter stood like he was itching for a fight, staring at Jim with those cold watery eyes, but all he said was, "Fine. You go your way and I'll go mine. But keep that kid and her dog away from my plane."

"I wasn't interested in your lousy plane. All I wanted to do was take some scenery pictures."

Jim's hand squeezed harder on my shoulder.

"Come on, Oriole," I said, turning away. "Let's go find some better air to breathe."

Oriole hadn't budged the whole time we stood there. I was relieved, hoping that meant she wouldn't attack someone even if they provoked her. It might be another story if someone came after me, though.

As Jim and I walked back to the waiting truck and his friend, he started to laugh.

"What's so funny?" I didn't see any humor in the situation.

"Nothing really." He coughed to suppress another laugh. "I'm just amazed at how you took him on. He would have scared away a lot of people, including most adults."

"Yeah, well, nobody treats me like that. And nobody treats my dog like that, either."

"Just be careful not to get too out of hand. You can't win with someone like him, no matter how right you are."

We reached the truck, and Jim introduced me to his friend. "George Halloway, meet Jessie Scott and Oriole."

George shook my hand firmly and reached down to pat Oriole. "I've never seen a yellow dog with markings like that."

"That's why I named her Oriole. She reminded me of one. And you should hear her sing."

Jim had retrieved our lunches from the plane and handed me mine as we loaded into the truck. Oriole settled down with her head on my lap and her body stretched out, taking up most of the back seat. "Where are we going?" I asked.

"To the ranger station. I'll sign the papers George brought for me and then we'll get your mom's CDs in the mail and exchange the batteries for her laptop, if that's okay with you."

"Sure. Oriole and I can visit everyone. And I brought my phone card with me to call my friends back in New Mexico. Wait 'til they hear what's been happening."

Spotted Bear was a lot quieter than before. The trail crews were all in the wilderness, so the only people there worked right at the station. Remembering Will, the boy I met the day we got to Spotted Bear, I banged on the door to his gingerbread house hoping he'd be home, but no one answered. Oriole and I went across the swinging bridge and down to the beach where she had nearly drowned. The river had dropped a lot, and there were no more rapids. It was safe to throw sticks for her in the water. She swam while I ate my lunch.

After lunch we went to our house. I replaced the used batteries for Mom's laptop with new ones and got some more CDs for her. Then we went to the office.

"Hi Cindy," I said, sticking my head in the door of the lobby. "How goes it?"

Cindy stood up from her desk behind the counter. "Hey, Jessie. Good to see you. And how's my favorite wilderness dog?" Oriole whined as she waited for Cindy to come outside to greet her. "Seeing Oriole makes my day. I get my dog fix from her."

Oriole seemed content to be pampered by Cindy while I called the Two J's in New Mexico from the phone outside the office door. June and Julie shrieked into the phone when they heard it was me. It was so much fun hearing their voices.

"It's been raining for days and days," June said.

"And we're sick of it," Julie added. "It's supposed to be desert here. Now we have to worry about flash floods."

"The mountains around Silver City have turned a beautiful green after all the rains."

"But what about you, Jessie? Are you having fun? Do you miss us?"

"Miss you? Why would I do that? And what are your names again?"

We laughed and laughed. I couldn't stop talking about all that had happened since leaving New Mexico. I told them about Oriole almost drowning, meeting Will and Allie, Hank Cooter, my scary ghost experience, and flying. When I finally said goodbye and hung up the phone, I realized that I was having fun and really loved Schafer Meadows. As much as I didn't want to admit it, Dad was right—everything would be okay.

With that knowledge, I walked into the office again, smiling. Rosie had come in while I was on the phone, looking very much like a district ranger and Dad's boss. She stood talking with Jim and George.

"There doesn't seem to be anything out of place in any of the houses," Rosie was saying, "but someone broke the padlock off the food cache and stole some of the food ready to go into the wilderness."

"When?" George asked.

"We're not sure. Probably either late last night or early this morning. Packer Brad Peters was supposed to take more food and supplies into Schafer tomorrow, but when the folks who work in the food cache went to get the food for him, they found a real mess. You can come see for yourselves if you'd like."

At the food cache I made Oriole sit just inside the door where she could see us but not get into trouble. We had to step carefully to not disturb anything. The place was trashed. It looked like someone had tossed bags of nuts, cans of vegetables, and boxes of noodles over their shoulder. Jars of jam and jelly, pickles, and mayonnaise lay broken on the floor. The cooler door stood wide open, and we gawked at squashed tomatoes, broken eggs, and ripped open cheese packages.

Rosie raised her hands in disgust. "Why would someone do such a thing? It's bad enough that they stole food, but it'll take a long time to clean up this mess. It puts our packing schedule back a few days, and we've got a full summer's worth of work already."

I don't know why but I got out my camera and started taking pictures. Maybe Mom and Dad would like to see them. "Were there any clues?"

"Not much. Someone left behind a partial print from a smooth-soled boot, probably a cowboy boot. But just about everyone wears cowboy boots around here, so that's not much help."

I took a photo of a print in some spilled flour. Whoever wore those boots had large wide feet. There was a small circle near the tip, probably from wear and tear.

Oriole sniffed around near the door. She couldn't reach the boot print without actually going inside the cache.

I got down and whispered to her. "Be careful. We don't want to mess up the crime scene. Too bad we won't be here. With your nose, I bet we could figure out who did this in a second."

"Is there any way to trace whoever did this?" Jim asked.

"I don't know," Rosie said. "Law enforcement's on the way. We'll see what they come up with. Meanwhile, keep your eyes open for anything that looks suspicious or out of place. It's always possible that whoever did this is still in the area. But please be careful and don't interfere. If you see anything, just give us a call. We'll take it from there."

"Right. And we'll have Tom call you from Schafer. You can fill him in on what's happened."

"Good, but have him call me on the satellite phone, not on the radio. We don't want anyone listening to this conversation."

"Okay. Well, we'd better get going if we want to get back to Schafer this afternoon. I'll have Tom call you when we get in."

George drove Jim, Oriole, and me back to the airstrip. Jim and George talked about the break-in at Spotted Bear. When we got to the plane, we said our goodbyes. George left to finish his camping trip, and we headed back to Schafer.

As we took off, it occurred to me that Hank Cooter's plane was no longer there. I hoped this would be the last we saw of him.

TEN

A Trail Mess

When we landed at Schafer Jim got Mom's CDs and batteries out of the plane and carried them to the house. He stopped abruptly just inside the door. "What's wrong, Kate?" he asked.

I walked inside behind Jim to find Mom crying. She blew her nose and wiped her eyes. "Felicia is devastated. Matthew just died."

I rolled my eyes. "Oh, is that all? For a minute I thought it was something really important."

Jim looked at me like I was the scum of the earth.

"No, hold on. You don't understand. Felicia and Matthew are characters from Mom's newest novel. Mom often cries when she kills someone off, especially if it's someone she really likes."

Jim sat down on the couch, ran his hands through his hair, and laughed. "Oh, man. What a relief! I'm really glad everyone is okay—everyone in your family, that is." He grinned at Mom. "And I'm sorry for your loss, Kate."

Mom sniffled and shook her head. "And I'm sorry to have worried you. It always surprises me how emotional I can get over my characters." She blew her nose one more time, laughed at herself, and took the CDs and batteries from Jim. "Thanks for delivering these. This helps a lot. Hey, what do you say we go to the cookhouse? I don't know about you two, but I could sure use a snack."

Oriole lay in the grass just beyond the porch, snapping at flies buzzing around her head. She jumped up and joined us.

Inside the cookhouse, Dad and Charlie pored over a map spread out on the kitchen table, discussing the trail crew's next work project. Jim grabbed a piece of banana bread and sat down to tell Dad about the break-in at the Spotted Bear food cache. I ate the last of Cody's cookies and gave Oriole a dog biscuit.

Dad called his boss, Rosie. He talked for a long time before he finally came back.

"Guess they haven't found anyone who stole from the food cache at Spotted Bear. Besides the ranger station staff, there aren't many folks around right now, just a few campers at the campground, a horse party by the airstrip, and a few other people along the river. Guess it's up to law enforcement now."

"Dad, did anyone talk to Hank Cooter? He was at the airstrip when we landed," I said.

"Hank Cooter? What was he doing there?"

"Don't know," Jim said. "I thought it was a little weird. He told me yesterday he was headed to Great Falls. Spotted Bear's in the opposite direction from Great Falls."

"Hey, you don't think he had anything to do with what happened at Spotted Bear do you?" I asked.

"No, he couldn't have," Dad said. "He flew out of Schafer this morning. The break-in at the food cache took place before he left. Rosie said they'll keep searching Spotted Bear for whoever did this, but she wants us to stay alert here, too. She said to keep our eyes open for anyone who looks out of place or for anything that doesn't seem right."

Mom poured herself some iced tea. "Speaking of out of place, who moved my CDs? I had them on a corner of my desk next to my laptop. I didn't work on my story yesterday, and when I went to get a CD this morning, I had to hunt for them. I found them in the windowsill across the room."

I remembered seeing the light move around in our house at night and it gave me an idea. "It had to be the ghost. Dad and I didn't do it, and no one else has been in the house. Wow! This is really cool!"

"I doubt it was the ghost, Jessie. I probably moved them and just don't remember it. Nothing was lost, though. I hadn't put any more of my manuscript on CDs since you and Jim flew the last batch out to Spotted Bear. Guess I just need to be a little more careful with things."

We talked a while more, and then I went outside with Oriole. She started to wag her tail and bark excitedly. I stuck my head back in the door. "Hey everybody, Jed and Pete are back."

We went out to greet them.

"How'd it go?" Charlie asked.

Jed swung out of the saddle and patted Rocky on the neck. "Great. We made it to the trail crew camp with no problem. We had a little bit of time to work on the Miner Creek Trail so we stayed to help the crew. Good thing we did, too. There was a big jackpot on the trail."

"A jackpot? As in a pot of gold?" Jim asked.

"You pilots need to get with the backcountry lingo," Charlie said, smoothing out his white moustache with his thumb and forefinger. "Course I guess it doesn't matter much, 'cause you never walk anywhere you don't absolutely have to."

"Yeah, well you just remember that the next time you want to fly in my plane, old man. I'll make you walk." Jim's eyes lit up. He seemed to really enjoy teasing Charlie.

Charlie wasn't going to lose. "I'd probably get there faster by walking than by flying with you in that old bucket. Anyway, just so you know, a jackpot is a bunch of trees that have fallen on top of each other. Sometimes they're in a huge pile ten feet high or more."

"This one wasn't that high," Pete said, "but it sure was long. Must have been 40 feet or more along the trail. Jed got to use his crosscut saw skills. He held one end of the big saw and Cody held the other. They went through a lot of trees."

Jed nodded. "Yeah, that was really fun. Made me appreciate how hard the trail crew works, though. It took us the better part of two hours to clear that section of the trail. Cody and I raced Celie and Mandy to see who could cut through the most trees in ten minutes. Those two women sure can saw. They beat us by five trees."

"No surprise there," I said. "You've got such a weenie arm."

Jed took off his hat and playfully slapped my arm with it. "I'd sure like to see you take them on. You probably wouldn't get through one tree in an hour."

"I'd still get through one before you would."

"Okay, you two," Dad said, stroking Kitty's nose. Jed had taken her as one of the pack mules. "Let's get back to the trail work. Did you get any farther than the jackpot, Pete? I'm just wondering if there might be more."

"Celie sent Cody ahead to scout. He went about a mile or so and didn't find anything before he turned around. They're going to try to make it to the top of the trail tomorrow."

"I'll give them a call on the radio later. If it looks like they've got more jackpots, I may go help them out."

We folded the manty tarps and took them and the boxes and ropes into the basement. We stacked the boxes and manties in a corner and hung up the ropes. When everything was put away we helped carry Jed's sleeping bag and saddlebags to the house. Charlie and Jim took the horses and mules to the barn while Pete went to his room in the cookhouse.

"So did you meet anyone on the trail?" I asked.

"No. No one could get past the trees," Jed said. "If they tried, they'd have had to turn back and take the Schafer Creek Trail."

"So, Dad," I said. "Do you think I can go with you tomorrow if you go see Celie's crew?"

"Let me see what's happening first. I'll let you know after I've talked with Celie."

After supper Oriole and I played in the yard by the airstrip. She sat and faced the airstrip while I hid behind a tree. When I called her, she had to find me. I fooled her a few times by slinking to the other side of my hiding tree when she got close, but her nose usually led her right to me. Whenever she found me she jumped in the air and raced around the yard.

Later, Dad came and joined us. "I'm sending Pete out tomorrow to scout another trail that may need some work."

I couldn't hope that the answer would be "yes" to my next question. "I don't suppose you'd let me go with him?"

"No, but you'd better get a good night's sleep if you want to go with me."

"Wow, you mean it, Dad? I can go?"

"I talked with Celie on the radio and things are looking good but I'd like to check in with them, see how it's going. You might find what they're doing interesting—more so than just tagging along with Pete to look at some future trail projects. I want to make sure the jackpot the crew cleared is well back from the trail. Sometimes horses or mules spook when they see part of a cut off tree staring at them. We don't want anyone having a wreck."

I barely slept. I was up the minute I heard the wranglers call the horses and mules off the airstrip. At the cookhouse Mom fixed Dad and me a good breakfast, and Oriole got a bit more than she usually eats because she was going with us. Dad hoped to ride all the way to the top of the trail to inspect the crew's work and then go back with them to their camp, where we would spend the night. It would be a long day.

We left at seven. Red was ready to go, prancing around, wanting to trot. I had to hold him back. Dad rode Dillon and pulled Kitty behind him. Along with our gear, Kitty carried a saw, a shovel, and a tool called a Pulaski that has a hatchet on one side of the head and a small hoe on the other. Oriole raced up and back, up and back, checking out logs and brush along the way for squirrels or grouse.

We reached the jackpot about an hour later. The crew had cut a ton of lodgepole pine, Douglas-fir, and spruce trees from the trail and pulled them back far enough so they wouldn't catch on a mule's pack or scare the mule as it walked by. A couple of the larger trees measured four feet around. Dad saw only one small lodgepole that he thought might be a problem. He cut that one farther back from the trail and we hauled it into the woods.

Close to noon we hit the top. "Hey, look! There they are," I said. The trail crew sat eating their lunch in the shade of a tree next to a beautiful small lake. They did not look happy.

"What's wrong?" Dad asked.

"Look over there, Tom," Celie said. She pointed to a wide spot next to the lake, not far from where they ate. We got off our horses, left them with Mandy, and walked over there.

Empty food cans, paper, broken rope, orange peels, plastic sandwich bags, candy wrappers, and beer cans littered the grassy area next to the lake. Trampled red, blue, yellow, and white wildflowers lay flat and dying. A tree oozed sap where someone had thrown a hatchet or something at it. Beneath two trees the ground was bare and dusty where horses or mules, tied to the trees, had pawed in boredom. A huge fire ring sat right in the middle of the trail junction. It overflowed with partially burned logs, paper, tin foil, and more cans.

"I'd love to find whoever did this," Cody said. "I know law enforcement would, too. People have no idea how much trouble they cause when they do this type of thing."

Dad bent down and stirred the cans in the fire ring with a stick, sifting through the charred debris, hoping to find some kind of clue to whoever did this. "Well, not only that, but they also cause a lot of damage to the environment. Those trees now have open wounds that allow insects and diseases to get in easier, and it will take a while for vegetation to grow under them again."

Oriole sniffed under a tree about ten feet away in the woods. She came back with a white paper wrapper in her mouth. Blood from meat had soaked through it.

"Give me that, girl," I said.

I looked at the wrapper. Someone had written in a felt tip marker on the outside.

"Hey, Dad, look. This says *Schafer* on it. This must be from some of the food stolen from Spotted Bear. Good dog, Oriole. Good find."

"What are you talking about? What stolen food?" Celie asked.

Dad took the wrapper from Oriole. He told the crew about the break-in at the food cache and that meat intended for Schafer was among the stolen items.

"It sure looks like this is from the missing meat." Turning to Celie he said, "Unless you and your crew happened to bring some for lunch today."

Celie shook her head, her black braid swaying across her back. "No, we had no reason to. We only brought sandwiches and nuts and stuff for lunch. Besides, we wouldn't have thrown a wrapper into the woods."

"No, I didn't mean to imply that. I know you wouldn't do that. I'm just trying to figure out why a Schafer wrapper would be here. It looks like whoever stole the food must have come this way. Have you seen anyone at all on the trail?"

"Nope. No one."

"Well, if they didn't go back to Spotted Bear, they may be heading for Schafer Meadows. We'll have to keep an eye out for them. Meanwhile, Jessie and I will help you clean up this mess. We'll stay at your camp tonight and go back to Schafer tomorrow. When we leave, I want you to be extra careful. If you see anyone or anything suspicious, call me on the radio. If you can't reach me, call Spotted Bear. And above all, don't approach anyone or do anything to put yourselves in danger. If there's any trouble at all—any—I want you to go back to Schafer immediately."

"No problem," Celie said. "We thought the people who did this were just pigs, but now that we know they've stolen stuff, we'll stay away if we see them."

I walked all over the place, taking pictures of garbage, the meat wrapper, the fire ring, and even pictures of tracks, from both people and stock. One print from someone with large wide feet showed a circle near the top of a smooth boot, like someone had worn the boots a long time.

"Hey, Dad, look here. This matches the boot print from the photo I took in the food cache at Spotted Bear. I think we're onto something here."

"Could be, Jessie. Keep the photos in your camera until we can get them downloaded to look at closer."

"Okay. Hey, Oriole, come here."

I let her sniff the boot print this time, just in case she might pick up a scent.

We spent the next hour helping the trail crew clean up the area. We broke up the fire ring, throwing the rocks used to make it and the cold burned logs into the woods as far from the trail as possible. Celie and Cody took shovel loads of charcoal away and replaced it with fresh soil, trying to hide the fact that a fire ring had ever been there. At least whoever did this built the fire ring where nothing would catch on fire, even if it was in the middle of the trail where everyone had to walk around it. Mandy, Dad, and I scattered heavy rocks under the trees where the horses and mules had pawed the ground, hoping to keep other people from tying their animals to the trees, perpetuating the damage. Celie and Mandy worked just as hard as Dad and Cody. I tried to keep up with them. It was hard. We were all soaked with sweat.

Oriole had a great time, bringing sticks to everyone to throw for her, including some of the burned ones we had already tossed into the woods. She didn't leave anybody out. When it got too hot for her, she took a swim in the little lake.

Cody had made a "highline" for Dillon, Red, and Kitty while we ate lunch and cleaned up the site. He tied a rope between two trees about 12 feet apart and ten feet off the ground. He made three small nooses in the highline and tied our animals' ropes to them. He left enough slack in the rope so they could move their heads but not enough so they could eat the grass on the ground.

"I'm really pleased," Dad said. "This is exactly how I want you to tie horses and mules in the wilderness. The only damage here is from their hooves, and that's not much. The ground will recover quickly, and you didn't harm any trees. Let's put some small logs where Dillon, Red, and Kitty stood, and kick their 'horse apples' to break them apart or move them into the woods. Then let's try to get some of the trampled vegetation to stand upright again. The next party that passes by shouldn't even know we were here."

When we rode into camp about 5 p.m., Dad called Rosie at Spotted Bear on the satellite phone and told her about the mess the crew found, the meat wrapper intended for Schafer, and our efforts to clean up the area.

"Rosie's calling law enforcement on this one," Dad
said. "The wrapper that Oriole found pretty much confirms
that whoever stole the food from Spotted Bear is probably
somewhere in the wilderness near here. She stressed that we
should all be very careful." Dad turned to Celie. "I want you to
call me on the radio every evening until it's time for you and
the crew to return to Schafer. I need to know that you're all
safe. If you even suspect anything is wrong, you're to pack up
and head back to Schafer. I don't want any heroes."

"No problem."

Dad cooked a stir-fry dinner, letting everyone rest as
a reward for their hard work. Oriole ate while I pitched our
dome tent, staking it to the ground. I didn't want it to blow
away like we had happen once when we got caught in a sudden
windstorm in New Mexico. Chasing a tent that's rolling away
is not only hard work but embarrassing.

Later we all sat around in our camp chairs and watched
the horizon turn from light blue to dark blue to black. Stars
twinkled above the outline of the mountains. I grew sleepy
and called Oriole to bed. I had just started unzipping the tent
door when we heard a long, low, mournful howl like a lost dog
crying for its person.

"Wolves!" Cody said.

I'd never heard a wolf howl before. It was eerie, making
me shiver as the hair crawled up the back of my neck. But in
some ways it was also natural and welcome. We stopped what
we were doing and stood up straight, as if we could hear better
that way. Shortly, another more distant howl filled the night.
What a thrill! As we listened for more, Oriole stood next to our
tent, all four legs spread out. She lifted her head and returned
her best imitation of a howl.

We howled, too—with laughter.

ELEVEN

Law Dogs

The next morning while Dad fed and saddled our horses and mule, Cody got our gear ready to wrap in manties for the trip back to Schafer. I helped Celie with breakfast and lunch food. It seemed to take forever to eat, do dishes, and pack up, but finally Dad, Oriole, and I started back to Schafer Meadows, leaving the crew to finish their project.

We made good time. The shade of the lodgepole pines and a light breeze kept the sun from baking us. One large spruce tree had fallen across the trail near where the crew had cut the other trees. Dad sawed it out and we still got back to Schafer by lunchtime.

Mom was working intently on the computer, hoping to finish her manuscript for the next pack string out, so I said a quick "hi" and ran upstairs to shower. Oriole licked Mom's hand before curling up for a nap.

We'd only been gone overnight, but it felt great to get rid of the dust, sweat, and strong horse smell on my hands, face, and clothes.

I put on a Silver High Colts T-shirt, clean shorts, and running shoes before going back out the door with Oriole. I intended to take her for a brief swim in the river so she could get rid of her trail dust, but on the way there, we stopped to visit with Dad and Charlie, who were talking outside the cookhouse.

"Do you know Don Lightner, the new law enforcement officer for Spotted Bear?" Dad asked Charlie.

Charlie sat on a bench along the side of the cookhouse, mending a bridle with thin strips of leather he had cut from a tanned hide. "I've met him a time or two. Seems okay."

"Hey," I said. "Remember Will and Allie, the kids I met at Spotted Bear who are my age? That's gotta be Will's dad. He works in law enforcement. If he's anything like Will, you'll really like him."

"He's flying in here tomorrow. Rosie expects a lot of people through here in the next few days because of the pilots' association work weekend, but there'll probably be others here, too. Don's going undercover to see if he can spot our food-stealing culprits. Now, Jessie, you can't tell anyone about this."

"It's okay, Dad, who would I tell anyway?"

"I'm sure he'll tell the trail crew when they get back, but that's for him to decide."

"Don will fit in fine," Charlie said, finishing his bridle. "He flies his own plane and should look like just another pilot. And he's new so I doubt anyone will recognize him."

"Good. I'm too new myself—well, hey—look who's here."

Right then Oriole began barking excitedly and ran toward the trail. Pete hollered a hello as he rode by on his way to the back of the cookhouse. Charlie, Dad, and I went to help him with his animals and gear. Oriole's whole back end wagged when Pete dismounted and scratched her head. She always seemed glad to see her rescuer. She found a stick and dropped it at his feet so he could throw it for her.

"How'd your trail-scouting trip go?" Dad asked.

"Really well," Pete said, throwing a stick with all his might. "The trail's clear enough to travel through, but it could use some work by the crew to make it safer. How's everything here?"

"Let's just say it's been interesting."

Dad told Pete about our trip to visit the trail crew, the mess we found on the trail, and law enforcement's suspicions that the people who caused the mess were the ones who stole the food.

"We're pretty sure they're headed this way," Dad said. "Did you run into anyone on the trail?"

Pete lifted a heavy manty from one of the mules like it weighed nothing, walked a few feet away, and dropped it on the ground with a thud. A cloud of dust rose in the air. "Yeah, actually I did. One group of three guys is headed this way and two other groups said they were going to keep moving on. Two other men rode by later. I was in camp when they went by and didn't get a chance to ask them where they were going."

"Anybody or anything look strange or out of place?" Dad asked, taking the other manty pack from the mule, creating another dust cloud when he dropped it.

"No, not that I noticed. Well, come to think of it, the two guys I didn't talk to seemed in a hurry, but it was getting late in the day. They might have just been trying to get to wherever they were going before it got too late to find a decent campsite."

"Probably, but let me know if any of the people you saw show up here. We might want to visit with them."

"Sure. I can take a walk through the campground and the horse camp a mile upriver from here. Meanwhile, I've got a shower waiting for me."

Pete elbowed me a friendly hello, tossed another stick for Oriole, gathered his gear, and left for the bunkhouse. Oriole and I went down to the river, where we found a blue swimming hole shielded from the shore by willow bushes and deep enough for both of us. I had put my bathing suit on under my clothes in case I wanted to go into the water with Oriole. It was a hot, hot day, but even so, the water was freezing cold. Mountain rivers don't warm up very fast when their water comes from snowfields that melt slowly over the summer.

Oriole swam a long time, seemingly unaware of the cold, but the icy water took my breath away. I could stay in just long enough to get wet before leaving the river for the grassy shore with my teeth chattering. My skin tingled as the heat of the day met the coldness of the water drops rolling off my arms and legs. The river moved along, riffles sounding like small rapids. I let the sun dry me off while Oriole chased pieces of driftwood that I tossed into the cold water downstream from our swimming hole. She finally came out, shook herself, and lay down next to me to dry off. Soon she fell asleep.

Bees buzzed and a Wilson's warbler sang from the willows along the riverbank. Not a cloud invaded the blue sky. I looked down and Oriole twitched in her sleep. I ran my hand along her wet fur. She opened her eyes, raised her head in my direction, licked my hand, and once more put her head down and went to sleep. It was a perfect day.

My contentment came as a surprise. I realized how much Schafer Meadows and my new life here had become important to me. Sure, I still missed my friends in New Mexico a lot, but I was making friends here and knew I'd make even more when school started.

The thought of school brought my happy daydream to a screeching halt. I had too much to do here before school started, like hiking and riding in the mountains, exploring more of the Great Bear Wilderness, and discovering who was stealing food and messing up trails. Most of all, I needed to find out why the ghost was bothering me. It was time to get going. I jumped up, startling Oriole out of her sleep. We ran up the hill to the cookhouse.

We reached the top of the hill just in time to see Jim's plane take off. Dad, Jed, Charlie, and Mom stood at the airstrip fence waving goodbye as Jim nosed his plane into the sky. Oriole and I raced to the fence, but the plane was already getting smaller.

"Bummer! Why didn't anyone tell me Jim was leaving?"

Charlie leaned his arms on the fence. "We didn't get a chance to tell you because we didn't know where you were. But Jim wanted you to know he'll be back for the pilots' association work weekend. He wouldn't have left without saying goodbye if he hadn't planned to return."

That made me feel better. I really had fun with Jim. He seemed more like someone who lived at Schafer than a visitor.

Dad tilted his head toward the campground. "There's someone here you need to meet, Jessie. Two 'someones,' in fact. Let's take a walk."

A large tan and green dome tent in the campground stood next to a brown wooden picnic table by the trail. As we neared the campground, a black streak shot out from the tent and raced toward us. Oriole took off and dashed toward it. A black Labrador retriever about her height with bright white teeth and a long red tongue reached Oriole at the same time she reached it. Both dogs reared on their hind legs and body slammed each other, tails wagging heartily.

"Casey!" A man about Dad's size with sandy hair came out of the tent. "Casey! Come!"

The black Lab spun around and raced back to the man. "Sorry about that," he said, walking toward us. "I try to keep him from running out and scaring people, but he's so fast that sometimes I don't even know he's gone until it's too late. Looks like he and your dog like each other, though. Do you mind if they play?"

I had grabbed Oriole by the collar when the man had called Casey back. I let go and off she went after the Lab. "If you don't mind, I sure don't. Oriole hasn't met any dogs since she's been here. This is great for her."

"Casey needs this, too," the man said. "He works hard, but he likes to play even harder."

Oriole and Casey jumped on their hind legs again, batting

each other with their front paws, then dropping to all fours and mouthing each other's neck in mock battle. They rolled on the ground for a while growling playfully before racing off, Oriole chasing Casey and then visa versa. They got down on their elbows, rear ends up in the air, dog language meaning, "Let's play." Off they went again, chasing each other all over the campground and out to the airstrip.

Dad said, "Jessie, this is Don Lightner, the law enforcement officer for Spotted Bear. He's the one going undercover. Don, this is my daughter, Jessie."

We shook hands. It was hard for me to picture him as a law enforcement officer, or L.E.O., which is what the U.S. Forest Service calls its own policemen. Instead of the standard green Forest Service uniform with the law enforcement patch on his left shirt sleeve, a gun holster on his pants belt, and a radio microphone clipped to his shirt by his left shoulder, he wore jeans, a cowboy hat, sandals, and a Spotted Bear T-shirt. He didn't even wear dark sunglasses to hide his brown eyes. I thought all law enforcement people wore dark sunglasses.

Don watched the dogs, a huge grin on his face. "Casey's my police dog, trained to help me on law enforcement cases. That's how he got his name. You've heard of L.E.O.s being called 'law dogs?' Well, he's the real thing. What's your dog's name again?"

"Oriole."

"That's right, Oriole. I hope you don't mind if Casey spends time with her while we're here. He'll be one happy dog."

"Then there'll be two happy dogs. This is the most excited I've seen Oriole since we got here. She and Casey make a great team."

Don said he was thrilled to have another dog around. "It makes me look less like a law enforcement officer and more like just another pilot who came for the pilots' association work weekend."

"I'm surprised you've got a black Lab doing law enforcement work," Dad said. "I thought most dogs trained for that type of job are German shepherds."

"Most are. But some dogs, like Labs and golden retrievers, often specialize in sniffing out drugs, bombs, bodies, or similar work. Occasionally you'll find a dog like Casey who has the instincts and courage of a German shepherd for capturing criminals and can be used like one."

"He sure doesn't seem like he'd ever go after anybody," I said as Casey and Oriole circled us, nearly knocking Dad over. "Unless he wanted to play."

"Don't be fooled. He's trained to do whatever I ask of him, and he enjoys working." Don watched the two dogs romp and then looked at me. "I know you met my son, Will. Once this case is over, maybe Will can fly in here with me, maybe bring a couple of his friends."

"Yeah. I met Allie, too. She's great. It's good meeting people my age." I glanced at Dad, who still felt bad about taking me away from my friends in New Mexico. "But I've made some really great friends here who don't care how old I am."

Dad relaxed and smiled. His eyes showed gratitude. He could tell I really meant it.

While we talked and the dogs played, two men sat at a picnic table under a tarp. They didn't speak much. Dad suggested we go to the cookhouse. He didn't want the men to hear any conversation that might let them know Don was working undercover.

On our way to the cookhouse, Oriole and Casey raced in circles around us and then ran down to the river. I was sure Oriole would show Casey the entire ranger station compound, but only after they went for a swim to cool off. Oriole sure seemed to know how to take care of her friends.

🐾

That night I slept fitfully. Oriole lay stretched out beside me, softly snoring and twitching in her sleep. I heard Mom and Dad talking quietly in bed before they, too, drifted off to sleep. I tossed and turned, unable to lose the sense that someone was watching me. Could it be the ghost? Opening my eyes, I saw a man in my room wearing an old felt hat and torn clothing.

"What do you want from me?" I asked.

He stood and stared for a while, not saying anything.

"Why did you visit our house the other night? You scared me to death."

No response.

I wasn't afraid of him but I fell asleep not knowing what he wanted.

TWELVE

Another Mystery

The next morning, Charlie sat alone at the table in the
cookhouse, carving what looked like a horse or mule. His white
moustache moved with his hand, as if helping him whittle.

"Charlie," I asked hesitantly. "When Pete told us about
the ghost of Schafer Meadows, he didn't say who he thought it
was. Do you have any ideas?"

"Why do you ask?"

"Just wondering." I felt kind of silly talking about a ghost.
After all, I'd never believed in them and didn't want to tell
Charlie I thought one actually visited me.

Charlie put down his knife and wooden sculpture. "If
there is a ghost, it's most likely William Schafer."

"Who's that? Did they name Schafer Meadows after him?"

"They did. He supposedly built a cabin upriver near
what's now called the 'horse camp.' Schafer was a trapper here
before most people even knew about this country, probably
trapping beaver and small animals like pine martens for their
fur. He was found shot in his cabin in 1908."

"Wow! Did they ever find out who did it?"

"No one was ever charged. There's a good chance he was
killed over trapping rights. Trapping was pretty big stuff back
then. Furs could be worth a lot of money."

"So you think Schafer's ghost could be wandering around
because his killer was never caught?"

"Maybe. Who knows, Jessie? It's all in the past."

"Yeah, you're right. You gotta admit that it makes a great
story, though."

I left Charlie sitting at the table with his white-haired head bent over his sculpture, which looked more and more like a mule wearing packs.

The next two days were great. Oriole and Casey played, and Jed and I spent a lot of time with Dad, Charlie, and Don while they worked out a game plan for Don's undercover operation. Mom continued to write her book. Packer Brad returned with his mule train loaded with food for us and hay and grain for the horses and mules. He also brought Mom some recharged batteries. She went through them fast but never missed a day of writing because of a dead battery. The Schafer Meadows-to-Spotted Bear "Pony Express" worked slick for her.

People came and went, some who backpacked a night or two at the campground, some who flew into Schafer to float the river out, and some who trickled in to spend a couple of extra days before the pilots' work weekend began. Don sent Pete through the campground and up the trail to the horse camp to see if he recognized anyone from when he was scouting trail work.

"No one in the campground looks familiar," Pete said, "but I recognize two groups at the horse camp, one with three men and one with two."

"How'd they seem?" Don asked. Pete, Dad, Don and I were sitting around the sunny picnic table outside the cookhouse enjoying a cold glass of lemonade.

"The three guys seem okay. They came to fish and hang out for a few days before continuing on an extended trip. They want to be gone before the pilots come in. Those other two guys were kinda weird, though. They weren't unfriendly, just not very talkative. And I had to get them to clean up their campsite. It was a mess—empty cans, open food containers, and personal gear strewn all over the place. I had to remind them that there are grizzly bears and other critters who would love to share their food. When I explained that they needed to store their food in bear-proof boxes or hang it in trees to keep it out of the reach of bears, they seemed unaware that they needed to worry about that."

"Did you get any names?" Dad asked.

"The three anglers were Bill, Dave, and Tony, all from Missoula. The other two were Doug and Les. Said they're from Kalispell and don't know how long they'll be here, maybe a week or more."

"Know what they're doing here?"

"Said they're just taking time off work to relax a bit. Didn't look like they came to fish—at least I didn't see any fishing gear—and they don't look like the hiking or riding type. I think they just plan to hang around and drink beer."

Dad rolled his eyes. "Wonderful. I just hope they don't cause any trouble."

"And another thing, Tom. They're the ones who set up the tarp in the campground. They're staying at the horse camp about a mile from here, but they hang out in the campground. I don't get it. I wouldn't want to leave my horses and mules alone all day while I hung out somewhere else."

"Yeah, you're right. We may need to watch those two."

Don turned his lemonade glass around and around in his hands. "I'll probably be the best one to do that. I'll be at the campground quite a bit and can keep a pretty close eye on them when they hang around under their tarp. Tom and Pete, when they go to the horse camp, I think you should be the ones who visit them. They know it's your job to do that and may be less suspicious that way."

Jed came by and asked if I wanted to ride with him around Lodgepole Mountain. Oriole and Casey were sacked out under the picnic table, showing no signs of movement. We went to the barn to get Red and Rocky, talking about Don and the undercover operation. Both of us thought it was pretty exciting.

"I saw those two guys, Les and Doug," Jed said. "I took a walk to the horse camp just to stretch. They were taking their horses and mules down to the river for water. They didn't seem to want to talk to me."

"So what makes you think anyone would want to talk to you?" I hadn't had a chance to kid Jed for a while.

"Oh, go suck an egg." He whapped me lightly on the back of the head in retaliation and ran. I raced after him, but he was way faster.

"Huh," he said when I reached him. He stood by the grain shed next to the barn, holding the door open and looking inside the door. "Some pack rat or something must have gotten into the grain."

A large bag lay open on its side. Grain had spilled onto the floor. "I helped Packer Brad store all the grain when he brought it in last time. I know it was in good shape when we left."

I walked inside the small room. "Could that bag have slid off the others and onto the floor?"

Jed shrugged. "It's possible, but we had the bags well stacked." He took off his cowboy hat, ran his fingers through his hair, and put his hat back on. "The door was slightly open when I got here. You know we're careful to keep it closed so nothing can get inside. It's possible somebody could have come in if we forgot to lock the door. Hard to say if anyone took any of the grain."

"Why would someone do that? Hey, I bet it was the ghost. There seem to be more and more unexplained things happening all the time."

"You really starting to believe in all that ghost business?"

I felt a little embarrassed. Covering my tracks, I said, "Not really, but what else could it be?"

"I don't know. Guess we should tell Dad and Don. Looks like there's one more mystery to add to their list."

THIRTEEN

The Snack

Plane after plane, most holding two to four people, landed on the airstrip as Jed and I returned from our ride to Lodgepole Mountain and put Rocky and Red in the corral. Yellow, red, blue, and green planes colored the ground. So many came in that I didn't think they'd ever stop. The next day the pilots' association work weekend would start.

"Hey, Jed," I said, watching yet another airplane land. "Do you think it might cause a problem with so many planes coming in for the weekend?"

When we first got to Schafer, Rosie, Dad's boss, said only a few airstrips exist in any wilderness in the whole country. "We have a limit we try not to exceed," she had said, "and if we ever get to the place where we have too many planes flying in, we may have to either allow only so many to land at Schafer or close the airstrip." I wondered if having this many planes at one time might cause the airstrip to eventually close.

"I asked Dad about that," Jed said, "and he said they keep close tabs on how many come in, but so far they haven't gone over the total number of aircraft allowed in a year."

Pilots tied their planes just off the runway. It looked like a mini airport. Some pilots pitched tents next to their plane and others put theirs up in the campground. Smoke from campfires rose to the sky. A makeshift kitchen covered by tarps took up one end, and gas camp stoves sat on the ends of tables. Steaming pots smelled of chili and stew. I wandered

around with Mom and Dad, meeting people and eyeballing
the food. There was a ton of it. There must have been at least
forty people there, and they weren't going to starve over the
weekend.

The next day was the 4th of July, and, except for eating
ourselves to death, I wasn't sure how we would celebrate.
Fireworks aren't allowed in the wilderness.

I kept looking for kids my age, but there weren't any. It
didn't matter much, though, because the trail crew was back.
Celie, Cody, and Mandy had come back to help the pilots with
their work projects. Mom and Dad talked with the pilots, and
Oriole and I visited with Don and Casey. For once the two dogs
were content to just sit together and watch people.

I was so engrossed in all the food that my favorite plane
landed without me knowing it. Not until I heard my name
did I realize that Jim had returned. Oriole jumped up, leaving
Casey and wagging her way over to Jim in hopes of gaining his
affections and a treat. It worked.

Jim held out two paper bags, letting her sniff them. "Pick
your bag carefully," Jim told Oriole. "Whichever one you
choose is yours to keep."

Oriole's tail worked overtime as she smelled the bags.
Casey came up and wanted a piece of the action, too. Oriole
ignored one bag and nosed the other. Jim opened it and gave
her a rawhide bone. She bounded off with her prize.

Jim kept the bag open. "Who's Oriole's friend?"

"That's Casey. He belongs to Don Lightner."

Jim whispered. "Oh, yeah. The law enforcement officer
who has the law dog. He flew in the other day right before
I left. I didn't recognize Casey. Guess I'll have to get better
acquainted with those two. Starting with this good dog."

He reached into the bag, pulling out another rawhide bone.
He handed it to Casey who grabbed it and raced off in search
of Oriole.

Jim handed me the other bag. "This one's for you. Well, it's for you and Oriole."

I opened the bag and pulled out a red collapsible dog bowl.

"Thought you could take this for Oriole when she travels with you. I hear these are great for the backcountry. And it'll fit right into your backpack or Red's saddlebags."

"Oh, Jim, this is really neat! Her bowls have been old margarine containers. Now she'll be the envy of all backcountry dogs. I just hope she doesn't get a big head." I gave him a bear hug and we went to find Mom and Dad.

They were sitting at a picnic table talking with Don. I showed off Oriole's new bowl. We were about to go meet some more people when Mandy stormed up, her face beet red and her usually neat bushy brown hair sticking out everywhere.

"Who's been messing with my stuff?"

"What do you mean?" Dad said. "What stuff?"

"Cody, Celie, and I went into the bunkhouse when we got back from our work project and I found some of my things moved around in the bathroom."

"Did it look like anything was missing?"

"No. We all carefully checked our clothes and other gear but it didn't look like anything was gone".

"Are you sure some of your belongings were moved?"

"Sure I'm sure. I hung my towel and a bunch of laundry above the woodstove to dry the day we left for our work project. And I placed my shoes under a chair next to the stove. I'm sure because I sat there to take them off and put my boots on before we left. When we got back I found all my clothes on the other side of the room, tossed in a pile in a corner. And somebody threw my shoes into the other room where we sleep. I found one on a bed and one clear across the room on the floor. I don't like people going through my personal property."

"Did anybody else have things moved around?"

"No, just me. But nobody else had left anything by the stove."

Dad stared at the ground, thinking. "I don't know what to say, Mandy. Someone's been around the station the whole time you've been gone, and Pete's the only one who'd have a reason to go into the bunkhouse. I don't know who might have gone into the bunkhouse or why they would move your things around in the bathroom. And it's strange that they'd throw your shoes into the other room."

"Well, I'm telling you they did."

Don stood and walked over to Mandy, introducing himself. "Why don't you take me to the bunkhouse and we'll see if we can figure out what happened." He nodded to Dad. "And Tom, why don't you come, too."

They walked off to the bunkhouse. Mom and I sat stunned at the table. We couldn't imagine anyone going through her things while she was gone. It didn't make sense.

Unless.

I thought of the ghost. As far as I knew, no one had seen it but me since we came to Schafer, but there had definitely been things happening out of the ordinary. First, the ghost visited me in my room. Then I saw the light moving in our house that one night. Next Mom's CDs were moved around the day Jim and I flew to Spotted Bear. Then the ghost came to my room again. And what about the spilled grain in the barn? Jed was so sure it had been stored so it wouldn't fall. Maybe the ghost had been more active than any of us realized.

What was I saying? I didn't believe in ghosts. Did I? But then, how could these things happen?

All of this thinking and all of the food smells coming from the campground made me hungry.

"Come on, Oriole. Let's go to the cookhouse and find us a snack."

The kitchen inside the towering log cookhouse was empty. I hunted in the refrigerator for something to eat. Stale air blasted out, and carrots, cold mashed potatoes, and leftover soup didn't appeal to me. I decided to scavenge in the basement and hurried down the white-painted wood stairs.

When I reached the last step, I didn't know where to start. I'd never really looked around before. The basement was like a food warehouse. Two walls with white cabinets ran from the cold concrete floor to the wood-beamed ceiling. A thick wooden sliding door between the cabinets stood open to the outside where Packer Brad unloaded his mules when he supplied the cookhouse with food. A cool draft of air blew in, and I heard the cottonwood leaves shiver. After the discussion with Mandy about people moving things around, I wasn't about to close the door in case one of Celie's crew members or Charlie had left it open on purpose.

I looked in the cabinets. They were chock full of rice and sugar and nuts and individual boxes of pasta dinners and cookies and candy bars and energy bars. Under a window on another wall rested a long low freezer filled to the brim with vacuum-packed chicken, beef, and pork. Next to it was a refrigerator overflowing with cheese, veggies, tortillas, and whatever other foods wouldn't fit in the refrigerator upstairs.

The wall at the bottom of the stairs contained a thick white door with a heavy wooden arm. I lifted the arm and pulled the door open. It led into a room giving off the musty smell of earth. It was a giant root cellar, used to keep fresh food cool and away from sunlight.

"Whew. It's dark in there," I said. "Kinda creepy." I reached for Oriole, who had walked just close enough to the door to stick her nose inside. A flashlight hung from a holder by the door. I thought about taking it inside to see better, but my eyes had already started to adjust to the darkness. I left the flashlight and went in with Oriole at my heels.

A dirt floor dampened the sound of my feet. I slowly looked around. All four walls contained canned goods and glass jars full of pickles, spaghetti sauce, salsa, and other things, all marked with the year they were purchased. Some with dusty tops went back to 1998.

The center of the room had a small square wooden bench loaded with boxes that smelled of apples and oranges and soft grapefruit that needed to be eaten soon. Wire baskets hung from the ceiling, filled with eggs and cheese. Boxes on the floor were heaped with potatoes. Large round bins held flour. Oriole's little nose worked overtime, sniffing everywhere.

"Cool," I said. "I don't think we'll find a snack here, but this is sure fun to explore."

Just then the darkness closed in. I turned around in time to see the door close, cutting off all light. I heard the arm of the door slide slowly into place.

"Hey! What's going on?" I shouted. Oriole and I were in the farthest corner from the door. No one responded.

"Hey, it's not funny!"

No response.

I remembered that the door to the outside had been open when we had come downstairs. Had someone been in the basement and slipped outside when they heard us come down the stairs, only to sneak back in and lock us in the root cellar? No. No one would do that to me. It had to be the ghost!

Panic took hold of me. I grabbed Oriole's collar.

"Take me to the door, girl."

Oriole walked slowly through the darkness with me in tow. I walked gingerly along one wall with my free hand out, feeling cans and glass jars as we moved on. Finally finding the door, I pushed. It didn't open. I pushed harder, but nothing happened. I pounded on the door.

"Help! Anyone!"

The heavy concrete walls and dirt floor must have muffled my voice. Although we had plenty of air it seemed like I couldn't breathe. It felt like the walls were closing in on us.

Desperately I searched the door again, running my hands up and down, feeling its dimensions. My fingers touched a piece of metal near the edge of the door.

A latch.

Of course.

They wouldn't build a room where someone could smother. Unlike the heavy wooden arm outside, this one jutted into the room and could be grasped easily.

I lifted the latch. It moved. This time when I pushed the door, it opened with a whoosh. I exploded from the root cellar with Oriole by my side. The outer room was empty, but the outside door that had been open when we entered the basement was closed. Could the ghost still be nearby? I grabbed the handle to the heavy sliding door and pulled with all my strength. It slid open. Scared but determined, I looked both ways, but no one was outside. No sound came from upstairs, either.

Forgetting my snack and the open root cellar door, I bolted up the stairs and raced through the kitchen, thoughts of the Schafer ghost chasing me all the way.

FOURTEEN

The Storm

When we burst out the cookhouse door, I nearly ran right into Mom and Dad, who were walking back from the campground with Charlie, Don, and Casey. One look on my face told them something had happened.

"What's wrong, Jessie?" Mom asked. "Come to the picnic table and talk to us."

I grabbed Oriole and held on tightly. "No. I don't want to be anywhere near the cookhouse."

We went to the house, where I blurted everything out.

"I don't like this," Don said, sitting on the living room couch with his legs crossed. "Too many things are happening at once. Nobody working here would play a joke like that on Jessie. They know she wouldn't think it was funny. And I can't believe anyone here would toss Mandy's things around the bunkhouse."

He looked at me. "I'm sorry, Jessie, but I just don't believe a ghost did this. We do need to find out who did, though, and it's going to be tough this weekend because of all the people here." Don uncrossed his legs and sat forward with his arms resting on his knees and his hands clasped.

"Okay, here's an idea. I think it'd be best if we all work together. To keep my cover, I'm going to have to spend a lot of time working with the pilots." He looked at Dad. "Tom, can you go back and forth between the pilots and the campground?"

Dad nodded. "Sure. I can make it look like I'm helping wherever a hand is needed."

"Good. Kate, I could use you to help watch the campground, especially when Tom can't be there. Will that work?"

"No problem," Mom said. "I'm sure the cooks will be glad for some help."

"Okay, then. Charlie, can you keep tabs on the cookhouse and the ranger house?"

Charlie looked up from the small wooden mule he whittled. "That'll work. We need someone to monitor the radio over the weekend, especially with all the pilots here. I can do that from the cookhouse and watch the ranger house at the same time."

"Fine. Then I'll ask Pete to take charge of the horse camp and let's have the trail crew stick around just to watch for anything unusual. We'll see if we can't figure out what's happening."

"What about me?" I said. "I can help. So can Oriole."

"I don't want you to get too involved with this, Jessie. Same with your brother, Jed. You can keep your eyes open, but if you see or hear anything, I want to you tell me, your parents, or Charlie right away. You can help me keep my cover by letting Oriole play with Casey. Speaking of which, I'd like Casey to check out the barn, bunkhouse, and cookhouse for smells."

"Can Oriole and I come with you? I'd like to see how Casey works. Maybe Oriole can learn something."

"Sure. In fact, that's a great idea. If someone is watching, we can make it look like you're taking me on a tour."

Don and I went off together with Oriole and Casey. The two dogs played as we walked around. They only stopped when they were inside the buildings where no one could see or hear Don give Casey commands to smell the area. Casey didn't find anything unusual. Once back outside, the dogs were off playing again. When we finished, Don said that was all that we could do unless something else happened.

The rest of the day was relatively quiet. Dad, Pete, and Celie met with the people from the pilots' association to discuss the fence-mending and outhouse-building projects laid out for the weekend. Some pilots and spouses who flew in to work visited the cookhouse where Charlie gave them a cold drink, hot coffee, or tea. Some fished along the river. Still others sat in their lawn chairs by their campsites, laughing and talking.

Les and Doug, the two guys with the tarp in the campground, just sat and sat and sat, smoking and drinking beer.

The pilots invited us for dinner in the campground, so I helped Charlie bake a vanilla sheet cake with white icing big enough to feed 50 people. Oriole slept under the dining room table.

Don had asked everyone helping him to meet briefly before dinner so we could share anything we might have found. Mom, Dad, Jed, and Celie slowly worked their way into the cookhouse. Finally Mandy, Pete, and Cody came in, followed by Don and Casey. We met around the table, keeping the door open in case anyone came by. Don wanted this conversation to be private. Charlie whittled his mule while half facing the door so he could see anyone coming our way.

"So. Before we begin, I want to tell all of you that what happened to Mandy and Jessie is inexcusable," Don said.

I thought about my experience with Oriole in the basement root cellar. It made my scalp tingle again just thinking of it. Mandy must have felt awful having someone go through her belongings and throw them around.

"Living together at Schafer means respecting each other. We all know that none of us did this, so who did? And why?

We'll figure it out, but we all need to help. Now, does anyone have anything to report?"

The only one who did was Pete, who said three more groups arrived at the horse camp. Nothing seemed out of the ordinary with them, though.

"Well, let's keep close watch tonight and over the weekend. And be careful. I don't want any of you doing anything that could get you into trouble or make someone suspicious. If you have reason to believe something is wrong or there could be danger, drop what you're doing and find me right away."

After that, we sat around the table listening to the crew tell tales about what happened on their first trail project. Then someone asked Don if he'd heard if the jewel robbery from the Kalispell mall had been solved. Don said the police were still hunting for the thieves. They had few leads.

One of the pilots came to the door, saying dinner would be served in half an hour at the campground. We hurried home to get sweatshirts and flashlights for the evening.

Late that night it stormed. The wind howled, rattling the windows in our snug house. Lightning flashed, first far away and then nearer and nearer, until it seemed to be everywhere at once. Some bolts streaked from one cloud to another, lighting the night sky, while others shot from black clouds to the ground. Thunder rolled in with the lightning. Loud booms shook our home as lightning bolts nearest the house hit the ground. Sheets of rain battered the roof and hammered the windows.

Somewhere far off came the frightened neighing of horses and then pounding hooves as the horses galloped on the trail behind the cookhouse. I knew they weren't ours—they'd be on the airstrip—so someone from the horse camp a mile away from Schafer would probably be out chasing their animals the next morning, hoping they didn't run very far in the night and wishing they'd secured them better before the storm.

I felt sorry for all the animals out in the storm. I lay in bed, holding tightly to Oriole. Many dogs have a terrible fear of loud noises, cowering and shivering or frantically searching for a safe place to hide. Some even run away and get lost. Oriole didn't seem the least bit concerned about the terrible weather, even snoring through some of it. I hoped she would never gain that fear.

I got up from my bed and went to the stairs to look out the window that faced the cookhouse. A flash of lightning showed someone walking from the cookhouse toward the bunkhouse. It was a terrible time to be outside. The rain came in torrents. Maybe Pete was going off to bed, but I doubted it. It didn't look like anyone from the ranger station.

As the hard rain continued to fall, another flash of lightning showed the phantom form of a large man walking away. That strangling fear took hold of me again. My stomach rolled thinking of the ghost on the prowl. Was it looking for something? Snooping around to scare me? Or was it really only one of the pilots who just happened to get caught in the rain?

The lightning flashed again, and it was gone. Had I seen the ghost? I crept back to bed and held even tighter to Oriole, falling asleep at last, feeling snug and safe with her.

FIFTEEN

A Ghostly Intruder

Morning dawned as if the storm had never happened. I awoke to a bright sunny day with big puffy clouds. The air was a lot cooler than the day before. It would be a good day for the work weekend.

"Don't you love the wet earthy smell after a good storm, Oriole?"

She cocked her head to show her black ear and eye and wagged her tail.

Glancing at the airstrip on our way to the cookhouse for breakfast, I saw that all the planes remained securely tied to the ground. The pilots had protected their planes from the winds of the storm. None showed any sign of damage.

I looked for footprints outside the cookhouse. Most of the walkway had gravel, so there weren't any tracks. Where the ground was dirt the rain had soaked through, leaving lots of footprints. It looked like a herd of elephants had stomped through there. I couldn't tell one print from another. There'd be no way to know which ones belonged to the ghost—if a ghost left tracks, that is.

I ate breakfast with Mom, Charlie, and Jed. Everyone else was already out working. Someone knocked on the door.

"Happy 4th of July!" Charlie said, opening the door. "Come on in."

Two men stood just inside the door, glancing about. I recognized them as the men who sat all day under the tarp in the campground.

Charlie stuck out his hand in welcome. "I'm Charlie, and this is Kate, Jed, and Jessie."

The man with a pot belly, big jowls, and an old torn flannel shirt took Charlie's hand.

"Les Quincy."

The other man with thin hair and pants that hung below his waist reached for Charlie's hand next.

"Doug Frampton. Say, nice cook stove. I ain't seen one o' them in a long time. Mind if I take a look? I used to work at a place that sold antiques."

He walked to the stove and ran his hand over the metal doors. Then he opened the oven and peered inside, looking down, then toward the back, and then tilting his head to see the top. He ran his hand inside the stove as if inspecting it. "Nice. Really nice. You sure keep this in good order." He closed the door and went to stand by Les.

"Have a cup of coffee," Mom said, bringing over a fresh pot from the stove. "Cups are on the table."

"Thanks but no thanks, ma'am," Doug said. "We lost our stock in the storm last night when our tent blowed over. They freaked out and run off. We was hopin' you mighta seen 'em come this way."

The door opened and Pete stuck his head in. "Are you two looking for some horses and mules?"

Les nodded. "We are."

"Thought you might. Found them down by the river about fifteen minutes ago, hanging out under a cottonwood tree."

"Thanks," Les said. He turned back toward Mom. "Well, better be going."

"Don't feel like you have to run off," Mom said. "We'll have a cup of coffee ready when you come back through with your animals."

"Nope. Don't mean to be rude but we better get the stock back to camp. And we gotta put our tent back up in case it rains again."

The two men walked out the door and left.

"Most people who come in here want to stay and visit," Charlie said. "Don't know why they were in such a hurry. They could have brought their animals back here once they got them, and it's not like the rain's going to fall from the sky anytime soon." Charlie washed another dish and put it in the rack to dry. "Aw, who knows? Maybe they're okay. It's hard to second-guess people."

Oriole and I worked our way to the campground. Not long afterwards, Les and Doug came through with their horses and mules. They led their animals past the campground toward the horse camp.

Later in the day I took Oriole along the Big River Trail to the horse camp, thinking I'd do some birding and snooping at the same time with my high-powered birding binoculars. Les and Doug were pounding in their tent stakes.

"Hey, there," I said. "You guys must've had a rough night after your tent blew over."

Both men jumped. They had been talking in low tones and didn't hear us come up. Neither man looked happy. "Sorry," I said. "I didn't mean to startle you."

"What're you doing here?" Les asked.

"Oh, Oriole and I have never been here before." I held up my binoculars. "Someone said this is a good place to see osprey."

I had no idea if there were osprey there, but they didn't need to know that.

"Don't know nothin' about no osprey," Doug said. "You might wander down by them other camps to see if anyone there knows about them birds."

"Yeah, I'll do that."

Oriole and I walked away. Those guys sure didn't want to talk.

We went to the other camps and visited with the people there, just to make conversation. All the while I kept my eye on Les and Doug. They finished staking their tent and took their gear inside. When they looked like they might leave, we hurried back to the campground ahead of them.

Nothing unusual happened the rest of the day. Les and Doug returned to their perch under the tarp in the campground. Dad walked around giving work orders. Mom helped cook in the campground. Don worked hard with the pilots on their projects, Casey played with Oriole and me, and Jed and the trail crew spent their time helping wherever the pilots needed muscle.

As I ate lunch in the cookhouse, Charlie stood hunched over the kitchen table, his arms buried up to his elbows in bread dough. The strong warm smell of baking bread filled the room from another couple loaves already in the oven.

Charlie had also fixed up a huge batch of potato salad. While I ate, he finished his wooden mule and put it in the windowsill with his other creations. The small mule and its manty packs looked real.

Jim had brought another surprise when he flew in, and he helped Mom and me hang red, white, and blue flags and streamers all over the inside of the cookhouse and our house. We wound streamers around the posts on our porch and the bunkhouse and took some to the campground. We strung streamers on the tarps over the picnic tables and put small American flags in bottles on the tables.

Jim stood back admiring our handiwork. "Schafer sure looks festive, doesn't it? A big city could hardly beat that."

Around 3 p.m. it rained again. This time it was more like a soft summer shower, and it lasted just long enough to keep the heat down. The pilots called a halt to their work. They wandered back to the campground to change clothes and relax.

At last we had dinner. We all stood in line for a huge picnic feed, with hamburgers and hot dogs cooked on a grill, salads, and lots of desserts. Mom made her famous red, white, and blue pie, a sheet pie with cherry on one side, peach in the middle (she could have made cheesecake for the white color but we like peach better), and blueberry on the other side. Doug and Les went through the line, too. The pilots must have invited them.

When we emptied our plates, we went back for watermelon. I didn't think I could ever eat again.

During the meal, Oriole and Casey wandered between tables, doing their part to keep bears away by chowing down whatever tidbits fell to the ground.

Mandy laughed as she watched them. "Look at those two. They're playing the crowd like experts."

The two dogs sat patiently by someone they hoped would drop food, staring them in the eye like they were starved, even smacking their lips and drooling on occasion.

Mandy snickered. "That's pathetic."

Both dogs got their fair share of meat that people couldn't finish, although I tried to keep Oriole close to me to monitor what she ate. Besides, I didn't want her turning into a beggar.

After dinner we sat around and talked. A few people played cards, and someone brought out a harmonica and played sad-sounding tunes. Celie built a campfire and I pulled my chair over to it. Darkness set in.

"Thanks for the fire, Celie," Jim said. "Sure feels good, and the wood smoke smells great."

Charlie returned to the station, and Les and Doug left their tarp and walked off slowly to the horse camp. They didn't bother to thank the pilots for dinner.

I enjoyed sitting around the campfire, watching the yellow-orange firelight flicker on the campers' faces. Oriole and Casey chased each other through the campground until they had their fill of play, and when Oriole came to lie down next to me, Casey went to find Don.

Mom came and sat down next to me. "Did you have a fun 4th of July, Jessie?"

"I did, Mom, but watching the logs spit sparks made me wonder if the Two J's are at the fireworks in Silver City right now. I miss them."

"I know you do, and I'm sorry."

"It's okay. I'm getting used to them not being here and me not being there. I guess making some good friends has made me feel better."

The cool rain and the hot sun of the day had created just the right mixture for fog. As the night wore on, a fogbank crept across the airstrip until it engulfed us by the campfire. It created a halo around us as we sat there talking into the night. My face felt cool and damp from misty droplets the fog made. A cup of hot cocoa kept me warm but later when it started getting chilly, I got sleepy and wanted to go back to the house to bed. Mom said she didn't want me going back alone. I told her that Oriole wouldn't let anything happen to me. Mom reluctantly agreed to let me go. She said she and Dad would be along shortly.

My flashlight stayed in my pocket as we walked back. I knew the way by heart, and Oriole could lead us if I got off the trail. The dense fog made walking back slow. I nearly jumped out of my skin when we reached the bunkhouse. It appeared suddenly. It made me think about the night Oriole and I stood by the bunkhouse watching the light move around in our house, and I paused to look. The fog hid the house, but I could see the vague outline of the porch light over the cookhouse door. Our house was dark.

I didn't light the gas lights in the house. Oriole and I went straight upstairs. My flashlight helped me find my pajamas. I went into the bathroom, brushed my teeth, and got into bed. Oriole jumped up next to me. My eyes got heavy and I fell asleep.

Sometime later, I slowly became aware that the screen door had squeaked open and then closed quietly. How long had I been asleep? Hours? Minutes? Oriole let out a muffled "woof." I shushed her and listened. It sounded like Jed's cowboy boots quietly moving about downstairs. Jed must have come back and was trying not to wake me. I heard the woodstove door open in the living room, then a rustling noise, and then the door closed. Had it gotten cold enough to build a fire?

Then I heard Jed's footsteps move softly into the kitchen. Why would he do that?

All at once my heart stopped. I realized it wasn't Jed downstairs. Someone else was in our house. I listened, afraid to breathe.

"Don't make any noise, Oriole," I whispered. I wanted to be able to hear every movement.

It was probably a man because the footsteps sounded heavy. He stayed for a while in the kitchen, standing in one place. I hoped he hadn't heard us. The scrape of metal against metal meant he must have pulled back one of the heavy iron lids on the cook stove. After a few seconds he slowly scraped the cover back on again. Then the footsteps left the kitchen.

I waited for the intruder to start up the stairs, ready to scream my lungs out and send Oriole after whoever was there. Instead, the footsteps walked to the front door, and the screen door squeaked open and then closed once more. As the footsteps quietly walked across the porch I slipped out of bed.

"Keep quiet, Oriole. Good dog."

We hurried down the stairs as fast as we could go without making noise. A screen from one window in the living room sat on the window ledge. Dad had repaired a tear in the screen and hadn't installed it yet. I moved it aside. The window was wide open. I grabbed a throw blanket off the couch, dropped it outside the window, and stepped through the window onto the porch, motioning for Oriole to follow. The blanket softened the sound of Oriole's toenails as she jumped down to the wooden porch.

We tiptoed cautiously onto the grass and looked toward the cookhouse. The fog had not let up. It was thick and hard to see through.

"Stay, Oriole."

We watched an image move slowly toward the cookhouse. The form of a man walked away from us, disappearing into the fog, the same form I watched walking at night during the thunderstorm. Now there was no doubt. It was the ghost!

Terror gripped me. I couldn't move or speak. In my dreams, the ghost was friendly, but it didn't seem that way now. Oriole wanted to go after it, but I clung tightly to her collar.

"No, girl. Keep quiet. We don't want it to know we're here. What if it turns on us and gets mad? Nobody's around."

We stayed that way for about five minutes, long after the ghost left. My legs felt weak. I was too afraid to return to the house alone but also too afraid to go back to the campground.

Finally voices came from the direction of the campground. Oriole's tail wagged and she whined for me to let her go. Mom, Dad, and Jed gradually appeared out of the fog. I let Oriole run to greet them.

I didn't want to tell them I'd seen the ghost because they always dismissed it as something else. It would be too hard on me if they didn't believe me again. But I also didn't want to hide anything from them that might be important. Thinking the ghost wouldn't come again that night, I made a quick decision to sleep on it and figure out what to tell them in the morning. A few hours weren't going to make any difference. Besides, with the darkness and the fog they couldn't do anything until later anyway.

Before they got to the house Oriole returned. I snatched the blanket off the porch, took it back into the house, put it on the couch, and then moved the screen back to its original spot on the window ledge.

Still pretty jumpy by the time Mom, Dad, and Jed got to the house, but not wanting them to see me so nervous, I took Oriole upstairs and got back into bed, pulling the covers up to my nose.

Mom and Dad came upstairs and stuck their heads in my door.

"Still awake?" Dad said. "Thought you'd be sound asleep by now."

"I couldn't sleep, so I took Oriole outside for a minute."

It wasn't exactly the truth, but it wasn't a lie, either.

"Well, try to sleep. We've got another big day tomorrow."

They both kissed me on my forehead and went to their room. Oriole tucked herself securely into my side, making me feel safe. It took a long time before sleep came again. For the rest of the night I kept waking up, sure I could hear the ghost.

SIXTEEN

Oriole's Note

When I awoke the next morning the house was quiet. I lay in bed for a while, thinking about the ghost. Oriole woke up, stretched, and yawned.

"You know, Oriole," I said quietly in case someone was still in the house. "I'm not afraid anymore. I'm mad. It's time to confront this ghost and tell it to leave us alone."

I needed to figure out what to do.

First, I had to tell my parents and Don about my experience last night. It was wrong not to tell them right away.

Feeling better after making that decision, I threw on a clean T-shirt and shorts and went to the cookhouse for breakfast. The sun shone brightly through the trees. The cookhouse was empty. The clock said 9:30. I had slept late.

I fed Oriole, got cereal from the cupboard, and went to the refrigerator for milk. Two boxes of big red strawberries sat on the top shelf. I inhaled their scent, grabbed a handful, and set my breakfast on the table as Charlie came in the door.

"Hey, Charlie—how's it going?" I said.

"Hey yourself. It's about time you got up."

"Yeah, I know. Had to get my beauty rest. Who brought the strawberries?"

"Take a guess."

"Jim."

"Right. He brought them over last night. He brought some for the pilots, but he wanted to make sure we got these for ourselves."

"Where is everyone?"

"Oh, they're all out and about finishing up projects."

"Are Mom and Dad around?"

"I think they're both at the campground."

I finished my breakfast and ran out the door. Near the barn an unfamiliar bird called. I hurried back to the house for my binoculars and bird book.

Oriole and I walked slowly toward the barn so we wouldn't disturb the bird that sounded somewhat like a robin yet not quite. The call came from beyond the barn, closer to the campground.

Suddenly a yellow flash shot past me and flew up the hill above the campground. Oriole and I followed the bird up the hill, finally finding it perched on a lodgepole pine, preening itself. It completely spread out one black wing with white stripes and bent its bright red head to pick at tiny insects. Then it shook its brilliant yellow body, spraying drops of water into the air. It must have just bathed in a puddle or the nearby creek. Thinking this would be an easy bird to identify, I sat on the ground and leafed through my bird book. A Western Tanager. No doubt. Cool! We had Western Tanagers where we lived in New Mexico, but I had never seen one before.

The bird finished cleaning itself and sang for a while before moving on to another tree. I was so caught up with watching it that it took a while to realize I could hear Les and Doug talking as they took down their tarp over the picnic table below. The sound carried well up the hill. They didn't seem to know I could hear them. And what they were saying caused me to listen—closely.

"I'm glad we can finally git outta here. I'm bored silly," Doug said, untying one end of the tarp.

Les untied another end. "Yeah, well, we better hurry. And he better be there on time. I don't want that stuff found in our possession."

"If he hadn't messed up that message, we'd of been long gone. Sure took long enough to figure out where to go."

"I know. But ya gotta admit it was pretty gutsy to stash them right under the ranger's nose."

Both men chuckled. "Yeah, that was pretty funny, but I don't like taking the heat for his plan. That horse trailer better be there waitin' for us. I still can't believe we got away without no one seein' us."

The two men folded the tarp and left for the horse camp. Oriole followed her nose down the hill to the picnic table Les and Doug had sat on for so long. She put her front paws on the bench and leaned out toward something white on the table top. A small piece of paper fluttered to the ground. Oriole raced after it and picked it up in her mouth.

"Whatcha got, girl?" I said. I looked up to make sure Doug and Les didn't see Oriole with the paper. They kept on walking.

Oriole tossed the paper in the air and caught it again.

"Bring me the paper."

Oriole acted like this was a great game. She ran around me with the paper dangling from her mouth.

"Bring it here," I said, more strongly. Oriole just stood there, wagging her tail.

"Oriole, come!"

This time she came and dropped the paper at my feet. Picking it up, I found tooth marks and dog slobber all over it. One corner was torn off. The paper was a note. It said:

"Look in _oo___o_e."

I tried to smooth out the places where tooth marks had broken through the paper, but Oriole had evidently destroyed some letters. The next line read "in the_____house."

What a weird note. It would take some time to figure it out. I looked for Mom, Dad, and Don, but didn't see them anywhere. Putting the note in my pocket, I decided to give "birding" one last try at the horse camp. Maybe Doug and Les had more to say, maybe even about the note. Maybe I could catch those dirty birds in the act.

When Oriole and I got to the camp, Doug and Les were packing up all of their food and gear. When they saw us coming, they covered up some of their things and quickly stood to meet us.

"Hey, how's it goin'?" I put my binoculars up to the sky. "Just trying to find that osprey again. You guys heading out today?"

"Looks that way, don't it?" Doug said.

"Where ya headed?"

"East side."

"Oh? How will you get your horses out if you came from Spotted Bear? You live on the east side of the mountains?"

"We got a pilot friend who had someone drive our horse trailer to the east side for us."

Les gave Doug a look that said he'd told me too much. He was right. I had a pretty good idea who that pilot might be. "Is it one of the pilots here?" I asked, knowing the answer.

Doug clammed up. "Nope."

"Oh, I know. It must have been Hank Cooter. He said he had friends coming in. You must be those friends." Just so they didn't think I knew too much and hoping to make them relax a bit I said, "He didn't like me or Oriole."

"Maybe that's because you ask too many questions," Les said. "You better go find your bird. We gotta git."

"Okay. Have a good trip out." I left with Oriole on my heels. We walked slowly down toward the river, away from their camp. I lifted my binoculars and searched the sky, pretending to look for an osprey.

After a while I got behind a tree where they couldn't see me and watched them through my binoculars.

Les bent over a manty tarp, wrapping one side securely before reaching for the other side. "Life's gonna be pretty darn good soon."

Doug stuffed a sandwich into a saddlebag. "You ain't just a-woofin'. Soon as we git rid of the stuff we'll be sittin' pretty."

When they uncovered the things they hadn't wanted me to see earlier, I looked closely through my binoculars. Another meat wrapper marked *Schafer* lay on a tarp. I now knew for certain that Les and Doug stole the food from Spotted Bear. But how would getting rid of the "stuff" make life good? What "stuff?" Food can't make life that good.

Les picked up some small drawstring pouches and put them inside a waist pack. He handed some to Doug and told him to do the same. "Keep 'em with you just in case the mules run off or something. Don't want to lose these babies. They're our ticket to happiness."

I didn't know what that meant, but it was definitely time to go find Mom, Dad, and Don. Oriole and I walked past Les and Doug, saying goodbye as we went. Oriole sniffed around and seemed particularly interested in a boot print—a large wide print from a soft sole with a small circle in the tip. I drew in my breath, realizing it probably came from the same boots I had photographed in the food cache at Spotted Bear and later when we found the trail mess. I tried to act relaxed as we passed by.

Wouldn't you know it? An osprey soared overhead as we left the horse camp. I didn't dare take time to watch it. But if Doug or Les knew I'd seen it and just walked away, they'd know something was wrong. I glanced back, but they were still packing.

On the mile walk back to the campground, I took out the note, trying to make sense of it.

"This must be the 'message' Doug and Les said 'he' messed up," I told Oriole. "Lucky you spotted it, but couldn't you have left your tooth marks out of it? They make it really difficult to figure out what it all means."

"Look in _oo___o_e" and "in the _____house."

Look in where? And what house? It had to be somewhere at Schafer. Was it the bunkhouse? Cookhouse? Our house? One thing was sure: Hank Cooter had left the note. I don't know how I knew, but I did. He had hidden something at Schafer and left it for them to find.

Suddenly it began to make sense. "Guess what, Oriole? We didn't see a ghost last night walking away from our house in the fog. It was either Doug or Les."

I laughed out loud. As silly as it seems, I felt better knowing that a real person, not a ghost, had searched our house. I should have been more frightened.

"What were they looking for and where? I wish you could talk to me, Oriole. Whatever it is could have been in the bunkhouse, cookhouse, or our house. But which one?"

I had to think harder about the first part of the note. Look in what? To figure that out I needed to search all three buildings.

When we reached the campground, I sat at the picnic table where Les and Doug had spent all their time. Once more I looked at the note. "Look in _oo___o_e." What was in the buildings that made a word with the letters that were still visible on the note?

Then it came to me.

Woodstove.

Could it mean "Look in woodstove?" There was one way to find out.

I forgot about talking to anyone about Les and Doug and went to the bunkhouse instead. Mandy invited me in.

"Hi," I said, trying to sound casual. "Have you seen my parents and Jed?"

"Not for a while, but they're around."

I glanced into the bathroom. "Hey. Can I see the woodstove in the bathroom? It sure looks different from any I've seen before."

"No problem."

The woodstove hadn't been used for a while. Someone had emptied the ashes, leaving the inside clean.

Thanking Mandy, Oriole and I left for the cookhouse. No one was there. I looked inside the woodstove even though it gets used all the time. It wouldn't make sense for Hank Cooter to hide something there.

Could the note refer to a *cook* stove, not a *wood*stove? I remembered that Doug checked out the cook stove the day he and Les lost their horses and stopped in the cookhouse. Because the stove was always in use, I didn't bother looking there.

Oriole and I ran to our house. It was the only place left to look. I stuck my arm inside the woodstove and heard the same rustling sound I'd heard last night when Doug or Les had been in the house. The stove held only wadded newspaper.

Next I checked the cook stove in the kitchen. I remembered hearing someone slide a lid off the top of the stove. I moved back one heavy round iron lid, peering inside over the hole it formed. It was too dark to see anything, so I ran my hand inside.

Nothing.

The lid clanged when set back in place. I lifted another lid. It also revealed nothing. Sliding my hand along the inside bottom, my fingers touched a small object in one corner. It felt like a piece of charcoal, but I picked it up and brought it out. A beautiful tiny blue stone sparkled in the room's light. I stood up, excited.

All of a sudden it all came together. I had to find my parents and Don.

SEVENTEEN

The Horse Camp

They were all there in the campground—Mom, Dad, Jed, Don, Pete, Jim, and Charlie. Dad was discussing where he was sending the crew on the next trail project.

"Sorry to interrupt, Dad, but this is important."

Dad looked up from the notes he had scribbled for the crew. "What's up, Jessie?"

"Last night I thought I heard the ghost in our house and then watched it leave. I should have told you then but didn't. What I really saw was either Doug or Les."

"What are you saying? They were in our house?"

"Yes. I didn't realize it at the time. And then this morning they talked in the campground, saying things that sounded weird, suspicious. They went to the horse camp right after that and Oriole found this note by their picnic table." I pulled it out of my pocket and gave it to Don. "We followed them to the horse camp to see if we might hear them say anything else."

Dad shook his head. "That was very dangerous, Jessie. You shouldn't have gone there alone."

"You shouldn't have gone there at all," Mom said.

"You're right, but it didn't seem that risky at the time. They thought I was looking for an osprey. Anyway, there was a boot print that matched the ones in my photos. It belonged to either Les or Doug. And when Oriole and I pretended to look for the osprey, I zoomed in with my binoculars and saw another meat wrapper and a couple of interesting little pouches. I also found out Hank Cooter knows Les and Doug and had their horse trailer delivered for them to the east side of the mountains."

I saved the best for last, pulling out the tiny stone that turned a dazzling blue, especially when the light hit it right.

"This came from the cook stove in the kitchen of our house. It's a good thing we can't use the stove. I'd have never found it."

Don took the blue stone from the palm of my hand, tilting it in the sun. "Whoa, look at this little beauty! I'm not much on gems but my wife loved sapphires, and I'm willing to bet this is a yogo sapphire. They're a brilliant blue like this and found only in Montana. Yogos are rarer than diamonds and extremely valuable, so this may be worth quite a bit."

"You mean they're worth more than diamonds?" Mom asked.

"Near perfect diamonds cost far more, but some large yogos can hold their own against them. In fact, it was rumored that the giant sapphire engagement ring that Prince Charles of England gave to Princess Diana was a yogo, but it turned out it wasn't."

I thought we were getting off track. "Hey! This gem may tie these two guys and Hank Cooter to the jewelry store robbery in Kalispell. Les and Doug talked about making sure they didn't lose the pouches, that they were their ticket to happiness. This little sapphire must have fallen out of one of the pouches."

"You may be right, Jessie," Don said. "If the jewels ended up here in Schafer Meadows, that would explain why it's been so hard to find any clues to the robbery."

"Yeah, but why bring the jewels here?" Jed asked.

Don put the gem securely in his pocket. "Hard to say. Why don't we just go to the horse camp and ask Les and Doug? I don't want everyone going, though. There may be trouble. Jed, you get the trail crew together and have them watch the trails. Tell Celie to have them keep track of everyone who comes and goes. They're not to stop anyone or talk to them more than they normally would. Tell them to just take good mental notes on who passes by, where they're going, and what they look like. If anything looks wrong, I want the crew to back off.

"Kate, you and Charlie stay at the station. Call Spotted Bear on the satellite phone and tell them what's happening here. Have them call the sheriff's office in Kalispell and send some deputies right now. Fly them in if possible. Meanwhile, monitor the radio carefully. If you have something important to tell me, call and say there's a visitor waiting for me at the station. That'll be my cue. I'll get out of earshot of Doug and Les before I talk with you so they won't hear anything we don't want them to hear.

"Jim, I know you're not a Forest Service employee, but would you mind staying at the campground in case the pilots wonder where we are? Just tell them some business popped up and we'll be back soon."

Jim nodded in agreement. "Happy to help."

"Great. Thanks. Pete and Tom, I'd like you to come with me to the horse camp in case I need help. Jessie, you come, too. You may have to identify some of their things. But I want you and Oriole to stay completely clear of the situation until I call you in. You mustn't go anywhere near those two. Do you understand?"

"I do."

Don called Casey and we left for the horse camp. It seemed a long walk there, but it only took about 20 minutes. Doug and Les had finished putting the last pack on the last mule and had just mounted their horses. Don told me and Oriole to stay on the trail just inside the trees, close enough so we could watch the action and hear what was being said, but far enough away to be safe.

"Let me start this off," Dad said to Don as they walked away from us. "They know me and Pete. It might make them less suspicious and nervous."

Oriole must have sensed something was about to happen because she whined and trembled excitedly. She kept her eyes on her buddy Casey as he trotted down the trail with Don.

Dad walked up to the two men. "Heading out already? I'd like you to get down and tie up your horses. I want to talk to you for a minute."

"We gotta get going," Les said, nudging his horse to a walk. "We're late meetin' a friend."

Pete stood in front of Les, forcing his horse to stop. "What's the rush? You've been here a long time doing nothing. Why the hurry now?"

"We forgot how long it'll take us to get out."

Dad stood next to Pete, making a barrier between Les and the trail. "Well, we need to inspect your camp before you leave. It'll just take a minute. Tie up and we'll get you out as soon as we can."

Doug and Les hesitated for a moment, looking like they might bolt, but they finally dismounted and tied up their horses and mules.

Don reached into his pocket and pulled out what looked like a wallet. He held it open to Les and Doug, revealing his law enforcement badge.

"What's this all about?" Doug asked. "You a cop? Why the badge if you're just checking our camp?"

"I need you two to sit on the ground and don't move. I want to see what you have in your waist packs."

Les and Doug looked at each other, but neither man sat.

"You got a search warrant?" Doug said, moving closer to Don.

Don pocketed his law enforcement badge and wallet. "Look, we can either wait until the sheriff's deputies arrive or we can get this over with now. Which will it be?"

"Neither," Doug said, and he took a swing at Don as Les sprinted past them. Don managed to block his fist and grab his arm, but Doug struggled to get loose. Dad and Pete caught him from behind and wrestled him to the ground before he could get away. They handcuffed Doug's arms behind him.

Don looked up to see Les getting farther and farther away. "Casey! Get him!"

Casey raced after Les, catching up to him as he neared our trail. Casey seized his pant leg with his teeth and started to yank him down.

Before I knew it, Oriole shot off to join Casey. She grabbed Les by his waist pack. The pack split open. A small pouch hit the ground and beautiful red, blue, green and diamond-like stones spilled out. Frantically, Les reached for them, but Oriole and Casey stood in front of him, their teeth bared. Les cringed and drew his arms and legs under him. "Get them off me!" he said, putting his arms over his ears to protect his head.

"Casey, off!" Don said. Casey backed away, and Oriole followed his lead.

Don stood over Les. "I wouldn't try to move if I were you. These two will eat you and spit you out again."

Les cowered on the ground while Don tied his hands behind him with a rope cut from a horse halter. Dad and Pete each took Doug by an arm to get him up and brought him over to where Les still sat. They gathered up the gems that spilled from the pouch onto the ground and gave the pouch to Don.

Don looked at Pete. "Call Kate and Charlie. Tell them we've got two suspects in custody and we'll be back to Schafer in half an hour or so. Jessie, would you get their horses and mules and bring them back to the station?"

"Sure thing," I said, glad to be able to do something. "Come on, Oriole. Let's go."

I tied the horses and mules together and led them down the trail behind the others. When we reached the ranger station, Mom and Jim came to meet us.

Mom said, "Charlie's on the radio with Spotted Bear. He said to tell you a plane should arrive shortly with three men from the sheriff's office on board."

"Perfect timing," Don said. "Thanks for getting the call in so fast. This'll save us a lot of time."

Don, Dad, and Pete marched Les and Doug into the cookhouse. The rest of us sat at the picnic table until a plane touched down and three men in sheriff's uniforms stepped out and came toward us.

Don held the cookhouse door open for the officers. "We can take it from here," he said as he disappeared inside.

Dad and Pete came out. We left Don with the officers and went to the house.

"That was more excitement than I want for a while," Pete said, collapsing on the couch.

"Yeah, me too," Dad said. "Les and Doug didn't look so tough when the sheriff's officers arrived. In fact, they looked pretty scared." He turned to me. "Jessie, I can't believe you figured out the mystery. You were great. And so was Oriole. Where did she learn to be a law dog?"

"I don't know. I didn't teach her. After playing with Casey so much she must have picked up on his cues." I bent down and gave Oriole a big hug. "You're amazing, girl. I'm so lucky to have you for my dog."

EIGHTEEN

Just Desserts

We stayed in the house for a long time while Don and the sheriff's officers interrogated Les and Doug. Finally Don came over to the house and sat on the couch with Pete. Casey curled up on a rug on the floor by his feet.

"Whew! That was some ordeal, but we finally got them to talk. They definitely took the food from the Spotted Bear food cache and were involved in the Kalispell jewel robbery. But before we know the whole story, we need to find Hank Cooter and bring him in. Les and Doug said he was to meet them once they got out of the wilderness, but it's going to be hard to find him. He flies a plane that looks like a lot of other planes. And he could be anywhere by now."

Jim, who had been leaning against a wall, said, "He said he was going to Great Falls. That was the day Jessie, Oriole, and I flew to Spotted Bear and saw him at the airstrip. Maybe he flew on to Great Falls when he left there."

I jumped up from my chair. "Hey, I almost forgot! I took photos at the Spotted Bear airstrip that day. A couple had Hank Cooter's plane in them. Maybe his tail numbers show."

I raced upstairs and got my digital camera. The photos of Cooter's plane came up but the pictures were too small to read the tail number.

Mom shook her head. "Too bad. If we had the software for your new camera downloaded to my computer, we could enlarge the photos. But we left the software at the house at Spotted Bear."

Jim moved away from the wall. "Is there a way to see if Jessie's software is compatible with any at the Forest Service office in Great Falls? If so, I can fly her there, get the pictures printed, and we can give them to the authorities to see if they can track down the plane at the Great Falls airport."

"Good idea," Don said, "except for one thing—it's the weekend. I'll have to see if anyone is working in the Great Falls office today." He got on his satellite phone and called. When he hung up he said, "The folks in dispatch there are working today because they have a small fire somewhere in the Little Belt Mountains and have sent some crews out to fight it. They called in their law enforcement officer because it might have been an arson fire. He said to come in and maybe he could help. How soon can you go, Jim?"

"If Jessie and her camera are ready, we can leave right now."

We were out the door. "Mind if Oriole comes along?" I asked.

"She certainly deserves another flight if she wants to come."

"What about Jed? Could he come, too? He loves to fly."

"Sure, go ask him."

When I asked Jed if he wanted to go with us, he nearly lost his cowboy hat as he dashed out the door.

"Thanks, Jessie. This is cool."

"Yeah, well don't say I never did anything for you."

In a couple of minutes we were in the air, headed for Great Falls. Jed rode up front with Jim, and I sat in the back with Oriole, who curled up and went to sleep. Once more the mountains filled the landscape and I had a hard time taking it all in. Peak after peak reached to the sky. We watched a pack string far below winding its way up a mountainside. The animals looked so tiny from the air. Farther on a waterfall plummeted to a small lake the color of turquoise. A tent sat in a meadow, and smoke rose lazily from a small campfire nearby.

One person lounged by the campfire while another fished the lake from the bank.

A short time later we flew past a sheer cliff wall that stretched for miles in both directions. "That's the Chinese Wall," Jim said. "Beautiful, isn't it?" Jed and I gawked at the enormous rocky mountain.

Finally we broke free of the mountains and looked off onto miles and miles of prairie, farmland, and grassy rolling hills. It was like going to another planet. Ranches, roads, and cars filled this land. Soon a city loomed in the distance. It got closer and closer.

"Great Falls," Jim said. "We'll be landing shortly. I'm sorry there were no snacks, beverages, or services due to the short duration of this flight, but I hope you enjoyed flying with Gunderson Airlines and will choose us again the next time you fly."

Jed laughed. "Hey. Gunderson beats any airline I've ever flown. That was spectacular!"

Andy Chesney, the main law enforcement officer for the Lewis and Clark National Forest office in Great Falls, met us at the airport. We drove the short distance through town to get to the office. It had been only a couple of weeks since I'd been in a city, but I felt incredibly out of place. Everyone seemed in a hurry. And everything looked so crowded—houses, stores, streets. Fast food restaurants, gas stations, furniture stores, and other businesses went on and on. Traffic slowed to a crawl as we waited at light after light. All at once my appreciation for Schafer Meadows skyrocketed. I was glad this was a short stop and I'd be going back there soon.

When we arrived at the Forest Service office, I left Oriole in Andy's vehicle in a shady spot with the windows wide open. We were met at the front desk by someone who worked for Andy. He hit a buzzer that allowed us into the main part of the building. It was a typical Forest Service office, with small rooms around the outer walls and large open areas in the interior where many people worked behind room dividers. I couldn't imagine myself working in a place like that. It seemed so distracting and impersonal.

Andy had his own office, and we all went in. He motioned for us to have a seat. "Make yourselves comfortable while I call Becky Stillman. She has the software on her computer to download the photos. You're in luck because she got called in today to make maps of the fire area."

A couple of minutes later we all trooped down the hall, went through another set of doors, and entered another small office. A young woman with glasses, dark hair, and a huge smile greeted us.

"Come on in. I hope I can help you download your pictures. Sometimes these things work and sometimes they're just different enough that they won't. Keep your fingers crossed."

I handed her my camera and she went to work. After a couple of minutes she looked up and smiled. "It's working. It should be just another minute or so. I'll save them to a file on my computer."

Finally the pictures stopped downloading. She turned her computer screen around so we could all see it. "I'm going to run the pictures as a slide show so you can see if there's anything you can use."

She clicked her mouse and the slide show began. It was really fun to see all of the pictures I took when Jim and I flew to Spotted Bear. "Hey. This new camera takes some pretty good photos," I said. "You never know how they'll turn out."

"Well, it looks like you must have taken a lot of photos in the past," Becky said. "There are some good ones here. Looks like you had a great day to fly."

Right then we saw the first of the photos I took on the Spotted Bear airstrip. There was the horse trailer and Hank

Cooter's plane with the mountains in the background. Not a bad photo, but we couldn't see any tail numbers on the plane. The next two photos were the same.

"Maybe I didn't get the numbers."

As the next photo came up, Jed pointed. "Looks like you got closer in this one. I think I can see some writing toward the back of the plane."

Becky stopped the slide show and went to the file where she had stored the pictures. She brought up that photo. "Hard to tell. Let me try to zoom in on the numbers."

Becky changed the size of the photo. We could no longer see the whole picture on her computer. She moved the mouse around until the back end of the plane came into view.

"Stop. Look there," Andy said. He pointed to some letters and numbers at the back of the plane. "Bingo!"

We all crowded a little closer to the computer. In clear print, we could see

N 0 4 8 I

Andy got on Becky's phone and dialed a number. "Yeah, hi," he said into the phone. "This is Andy Chesney from the Forest Service. The sheriff is waiting for my call. Tell him we've got a tail number for the plane he's trying to find. I'll fax him a photo of the plane with the tail number so he can see if the man he's looking for is at the Great Falls airport. Yeah, thanks. I will."

He hung up the phone. "The deputy said to tell you thanks for the good work. The sheriff's on his way to the airport now. C'mon. I'll run you out there so you can be on your way back to Schafer."

Andy printed off the photo of Cooter's plane and faxed a copy to the sheriff's office. Then we started back to the airport.

"By the time we get there they should have that guy in custody," Andy said. "Or at least they should know where his plane is so they can capture him when he comes for it."

At the airport the sheriff and his officers stood on the tarmac not far from our plane. Andy went to talk with them. When he came back, he said the plane wasn't there. Hank Cooter wasn't around.

"Huh. I'm sure he told me he was flying to Great Falls," Jim said. "I wonder what happened."

"I don't know, but they're turning their search back toward Kalispell where he lives. I'll let you know when they find him."

"Oh, well. We tried. Guess we might as well head back to Schafer."

"Yeah, well, thanks again for all of your help. We may not have gotten Hank Cooter yet, but we'll find him soon enough." Andy shook our hands and started to walk away. He turned around. "Oh, say. Would you mind making a stop at the airstrip in Choteau? We've got law enforcement officers at the Forest Service office in town ready to help the sheriff if needed. A photo of the plane might help them. I'd fax them a copy but their fax machine is down."

"No problem," Jim said. "It's on our way. Maybe we can grab some lunch before we go back to Schafer."

"Good. I'll call and have the Forest Service officers meet you at the airstrip."

A few minutes later we were back in the air, flying north to Choteau. We laughed at how the town's name was pronounced like *SHOW-toe.* Out my window the tops of the mountains zigzagged across the skyline in the far distance. Somewhere in those mountains sat Schafer Meadows and home.

Home. I didn't realize until right then how much Schafer had become home to me. I looked at Oriole, who lay in a ball with her nose buried in her tail. I felt like the luckiest person alive.

The plane's engine got quieter and the ground rose to meet us as we started to descend. We'd just gotten into the air. Choteau must have been a short hop from Great Falls.

"Not much of a flight," Jim said. "But I think you'll like this place. It's small and friendly."

We flew over a town with old brick and stone buildings on a main street and neat houses on tree-lined roads. The airstrip sat above the town on a bench. A couple of planes were tied up. We gently touched down. Jim taxied and brought the plane to a halt. We sat on the ground by the edge of the runway, waiting for the law enforcement officers. Oriole sniffed around.

All of a sudden Jed stood up, pulling his cowboy hat low on his forehead to block the sun from his eyes. He stared at the planes tied along the airstrip with a strange look on his face.

"No way."

"What?" I asked.

"What were the numbers on Hank Cooter's plane again?"

A small white plane was tied near the end of the runway. Jim said to me, "Where are the photos of the plane?"

"They're behind the back seat."

We hurried to the plane. Jim opened the compartment in the back and brought out the photos. "N048I. The numbers match. No question. That's Cooter's plane."

"Now what?" Jed asked.

"Now we wait for law enforcement to show up, hopefully soon. We can't do anything until they get here, and it doesn't look like Hank Cooter's around. He must have walked the few blocks into town."

Just then Oriole let out a low growl. Her hackles rose to form a stiff ridgeline along her back. We looked in the direction she faced and saw a stocky figure walking our way. It was Hank Cooter, and the sneer on his face seemed to grow as he got closer.

"I thought I got rid of you yo-yos a long time ago," he said. He started to walk to his plane but Oriole blocked his way.

"Move that mutt of yours or I'll move it for you."

"She's not a mutt, and she's not going anywhere."

"Jessie, do as he says," Jim said.

I couldn't believe what he said. How could we just let Hank Cooter go?

"Jessie, do it," Jim said, more forcefully now.

I didn't like it, but I called Oriole back to me. Cooter stopped right in front of me as he walked past. "'Bout time someone knocked some sense into that head of yours, missy. You and that dog are a menace."

Right then a Forest Service truck drove to the airstrip and pulled up next to our plane. Two men and two women got out.

One of the women looked from us to Hank Cooter. "What seems to be the problem?"

"No problem," Cooter said, looking bored. "I was just leaving when these people came up and started bothering me."

"We weren't bothering him," Jim said. "This here is Hank Cooter. He's who you're looking for."

Oriole began her low growl again. She stood behind Hank Cooter. I gave her a hand signal to lie down. She got on the ground, but she continued to growl.

"Tell that dog to shut up," Cooter said.

"Oriole, quiet." She stopped growling.

Hank Cooter shifted his eyes from one of us to the other and licked his lips nervously. He looked trapped.

"Get out of my way," he said suddenly, pushing past Jim and Jed as he moved toward his plane.

"Stay where you are, Mr. Cooter," said one of the officers.

Cooter broke into a run. For someone his age and size, he sure could move. He had put enough distance between his plane and our group to outrun any of us. I couldn't let that happen. I looked at Oriole. She stared intently at Cooter.

"Oriole! Get him!"

Oriole was up and running before I even finished the command. Hank Cooter reached his plane and had one leg up when she leaped up, grabbed him by the belt of his pants, and shook her head back and forth. Cooter reached back for the belt, lost his footing, and tried to hang on to the plane's door as Oriole pulled him backwards. His pants dropped to his ankles as he fell yelling to the ground. Oriole let go of his pants and stood over him, her face inches from his, her fangs in the biggest snarl I'd ever seen. She let out a deep rumbling growl as she put one paw on his chest.

Jed got there first. He straddled Cooter, pinning his arms to the ground. The officers caught up to Jed and handcuffed Cooter. They said they'd take it from there. Oriole still stood over Cooter.

"Oriole! Off!" I said. She backed off and returned to my side.

"Sit, girl."

Oriole sat next to me. I really had to try hard not to laugh as Cooter reached for his pants, which were still around his ankles. Who'd have thought he'd wear polka-dot boxer shorts? One of the officers, also holding back a laugh, pulled Cooter up off the ground. The smile disappeared and he became all business.

"You're staying right here with us until the sheriff arrives. He's got some questions for you about the jewel robbery in Kalispell."

Cooter still looked belligerent. "Yeah, well he can ask all he wants, but I don't know anything about that robbery. All I want to do is go home. I was on my way when you all showed up. Would have made it, too, if that dog hadn't grabbed me."

"Too bad for you," I said. "Guess I'll have to teach my dog not to be so harsh on people like you who only want to be her friend."

We waited around until a plane arrived and the sheriff and some deputies got out. The Forest Service law enforcement officers turned Hank Cooter over to him. The sheriff took his prisoner and started walking him to the plane. I was never so glad to see anyone go, but I had one more thing to say. I knew Mom really wouldn't like me doing this. In my mind I heard her say, "Jessie, you've got a mouth on you. You need to respect people." But how could I respect him after what he'd done?

Hank Cooter staggered past me with an officer on each arm. I yelled, "Hey Cooter. It's okay if you don't like me, but my dog doesn't deserve bad treatment. You thought you could outsmart her, but in the end you got what was coming to you. Mom calls that your 'just desserts.' I've got one thing to say to you."

All my pent-up anger finally found a release. I stomped up to Hank Cooter and looked him straight in the eye.

"Dogs rule! Thieves drool!"

NINETEEN

Top to Bottom

That night I again saw a man with a stubbly beard and torn clothing standing at the foot of my bed. He didn't stay long but smiled at me and touched his hand to his old felt cowboy hat in salute before he left. When I awoke I had the feeling that I'd never see him again.

Two days later we were all at breakfast—my parents, Jed, Charlie, Jim, Pete, and the trail crew—when the sound of a plane engine tore us away from our conversation. The Forest Service radio squawked in the office at the back of the cookhouse, and we heard the plane's pilot telling Spotted Bear he was on the ground at Schafer Meadows. We all abandoned our breakfast and spilled out the cookhouse door. Don had returned.

Casey jumped out of the plane and raced toward Oriole. The two dogs ran around, bowling each other over and playing like they hadn't seen each other in years.

I couldn't believe who else got out of the plane with Don. "Will! Allie!" I shouted, running toward them. "Wow, it's great to see you!"

"Yeah, you, too," Will said. He was even better looking than I remembered. "Dad said Allie and I could visit you now that the danger is over. I can't believe you caught those crooks!"

"Yeah, and I can't wait to hear the rest of the story from your dad."

In the cookhouse, Don said he wanted a cup of coffee. Casey and Oriole squeezed through the door just before it closed.

"I know you want the entire story," Don said, "but there's so much to tell. Let me start by saying we now know the identities of both the jewel robbers and the thieves who took food from Spotted Bear. As you know, Les and Doug were caught red-handed with jewels and food, and when the sheriff convinced them that it was to their benefit to talk, they told the whole story."

"Yeah, all right!" Jed slapped hands in a "high-five" with Celie, who sat next to him.

"Can you tell us what happened?" Mom asked.

"Sure. It's a long involved story, but I thought you might like to have some questions answered. This may take a while, though."

"No problem," Dad said. "No one's talked of anything else since this all happened, and the only way I'm to get any work out of my crew is if they hear the story from top to bottom."

"Okay then, here's what I know. Les and Doug moved to Montana a year ago after having gotten in trouble with the law in another state. They both had criminal records for theft and couldn't find jobs, although they didn't look that hard. One night, Hank Cooter sat in a bar where Les and Doug had also gone. Cooter heard them talking when they thought no one was listening. In low voices they laughed about stealing horse saddles and blankets from a store at night and how easily they had gotten away with it.

"Cooter already intended to rob the jewelry store in Kalispell but needed a good alibi and a way to steal the jewels without anyone being able to pick up his trail. He approached the men. He told them he heard their conversation. He said he could help them make big money if they wanted, or he could help the police solve a horse equipment robbery, linking the two men to the theft. Needless to say, Les and Doug listened to Cooter. Over the next few months, Cooter convinced them that they could pull off the robbery. Desperate for money and afraid of Cooter's hold over them with the police, they agreed to help him.

"On the day of the robbery, the jewelry store was full of people for a huge sale. The three men waited until the store had more people than the clerks could watch. When the owner went into the back of the store, Doug, Les, and Hank slipped in behind him. The owner had his back to them when they grabbed him. They blindfolded and gagged him and tied him up. Then they filled little pouches with as many jewels as they could grab fast. By the time the store clerks went to see why the owner was gone so long, the men had left by the back door and hurried to the parking lot where one of the local businesses was selling horse trailers."

"What about surveillance cameras?" Charlie asked. "Surely they would have caught the men on tape."

"The men disguised their looks in case they got caught on camera. They did a good enough job that even now, knowing what the men look like, the sheriff's officers who reviewed the tape couldn't identify them among all the other shoppers."

Pete looked up from his glass of juice. "Pretty cool trick. Okay. So they got out of the store without being caught, but don't tell me those guys bought a new trailer just so they could get away with the jewels."

"No, no. They already owned one. It was almost new and the same make as the trailers being sold, so it looked like they'd just bought theirs at the sale. No one would think them out of place driving away. Doug and Les had already given Hank Cooter their jewel pouches. Cooter took the gems and drove off to the county airport where his plane waited."

"Let me guess," Mandy said. "He flew into Schafer."

Don walked to the coffee pot for a refill. "Right."

"And that's when I met him," I said. "When he was so mean to Oriole and me before we even had time to say hello."

"Yep."

"But why did he pick Schafer?" Charlie asked.

"Cooter thought the best way to keep the police from finding the jewels was to keep them moving. He also figured everyone would be looking for a getaway car or truck. No one would suspect a plane or a couple of people on horseback. And he thought the police would search the towns in the area, not the Great Bear Wilderness. He knew Schafer Meadows had an airstrip and a lot of buildings, so when he flew into Schafer, he came to find a place to stash the jewels."

Dad looked confused. "But why pick the cook stove in our house? He had all sorts of places to choose from—the woods, other buildings that wouldn't have people coming and going all the time—lots of places."

"Actually," Don said, "your house wasn't the first place he chose. You know the 'bear boxes' in the campground? The ones campers use to store food so bears can't get to them? Cooter first thought of hiding the jewels there. The metal boxes open from the top down, and there's a lip that would hide the top of the box when opened. He thought of using duct tape to hold the pouches up under the top where no one could see them."

"So why didn't he do that?" Mom asked.

"The night he stayed in the campground, he ran into someone who told him about the pilots' work weekend."

Jim, who had sat quietly during Don's talk, said, "That'd be me. Remember I invited him to dinner that night and he didn't come? He asked all sorts of questions about the work weekend. He didn't seem like someone interested in helping out, so I thought his questions were a bit strange."

Don nodded. "Right. He had no intention of helping. He really wanted to know how many people would be around, and when he found out there might be 50 or more, he decided leaving the jewels in the bear boxes might be too risky."

"And leaving them in the cook stove in our house wasn't?" Mom said.

"It was. His second choice was someplace in the woods, but he didn't think Les and Doug were bright enough to figure out how to find them, so that was out. Then he thought about putting them somewhere else around the ranger station, like the cookhouse or bunkhouse, but too many people come and go from those places."

"But I'm usually in the ranger's house working on my book. You'd think that would scare him off going into our house." Mom said.

Don shook his head. "You know, sometimes crooks do things just for spite and because they think they're above the law. When Cooter first flew into Schafer and met Tom and Charlie at the cookhouse—"

"—And ate so many of Cody's cookies—" I added.

"Yes. Anyway, Cooter hates anyone with authority, so he took an instant dislike to everyone here. As ranger, Tom's in charge, so putting the jewels in the ranger's house, right under Tom's nose, was his way of getting back at all of you, showing how funny and clever he could be. You know, some crooks get so arrogant they think they won't ever get caught."

"Yeah," Jed said. "Look at Billy the Kid in the 1800s. He got into all sorts of trouble where we lived in New Mexico. I bet he never thought he'd end up behind bars."

"And he never thought he'd get shot later," Don said. "Cooter had that same overconfident attitude as Billy the Kid. He believed he was smarter than everyone else. To him, all of you were just a bunch of dumb government employees. He felt he could easily outsmart you. But he finally got caught."

"How'd he hide the jewels?" Charlie asked. "There always seemed to be someone around the cookhouse or bunkhouse. And like Kate said, she usually worked at the ranger's house. He'd have had a hard time getting past her unseen."

"Remember the night Jim invited everyone over for steaks and Cooter didn't come? That's the night he chose to hide the jewels."

"But we all saw him at the campground that night," Jed said. "He had his tent set up near his table and he sat with his back to us while we had dinner. How did he get in and out of our house unseen?"

"Did anyone remember seeing him leave the table?"
We all shook our heads.

"Wait a minute," I said. "I remember going to the outhouse. He was gone from his table but there was a light in his tent."

"Well, the police said Cooter waited until it was dark and you were all sitting around a campfire talking about the stars. He left his flashlight on in his tent hoping you'd think he was still in there. His tent door faced away from you, and he slipped out and walked as fast and far away as possible, hoping no one would see him. He walked in the dark, carrying a spare flashlight and not turning it on until he reached the house."

"He must have moved my CDs around in the house while looking for a place to hide the jewels that night," Mom said.

"That's what happened. Cooter first looked around your computer, but it didn't seem like a good place. He had to find somewhere else fast. He saw the cook stove in the kitchen, could tell from looking inside that it hadn't seen any use in ages, and made a quick decision to put the pouches of gems in there. It seemed like a safe bet at the time. It was summer, and he figured no one would fire up the stove until fall, if at all."

"He did like taking risks, didn't he?" Dad said. "Any of us could have walked back and seen him."

"I actually did," I said. "That was the night Oriole and I went back to the house alone and saw the light moving in the living room. I was so sure it was the ghost."

"Right," Pete said. "You came back and got me and we searched the house. Remember how Oriole's hackles went up and she growled?"

"Yeah. Now I know that she's only done that when Hank Cooter's been around. She must have smelled him. But how'd he get back to the campground unseen?"

"Same way he came," Don said. "By walking in the darkness and slipping unnoticed into his tent. For all you knew, he'd been there the whole time. All he had to do was wait until morning to fly out. No one would know a thing about the jewels."

"And he flew out to meet Les and Doug who were waiting at the airstrip at Spotted Bear?" Dad asked. "What was that all about?"

"Cooter's plan was to hide the jewels at Schafer, fly to Spotted Bear, and tell Les and Doug where to find them. Then he'd fly to Great Falls and wait.

"Meanwhile, Les and Doug would go to Schafer by horseback, get the jewels, and ride out to the east side of the mountains where their horse trailer was waiting for them. It would take them a couple of days to get out, but it didn't matter, because the jewels would still be on the move. Once Les and Doug got to their truck and trailer, they'd drive to Choteau. Cooter thought it would be better to meet them there than in Great Falls where they had more opportunity to run into the law."

"Why didn't Les and Doug just disappear with the jewels when they got them? Why did Cooter trust them to meet him?" Mom asked.

"By the time the robbery took place, Les and Doug knew how dangerous Cooter could be. He'd turn them into the police for their last robbery if they didn't follow through. They didn't want to mess with him, so they carried out their part of the bargain."

Pete reached for a banana in a bowl on the table. "Geez, what a complicated plan," he said, pulling back the banana skin.

"Yeah, but it didn't work out as expected," Don said. "Les and Doug weren't the most reliable people, and they caused some problems that led to their discovery."

"Like what?" Cody asked.

"Well, for starters, they got bored waiting for Cooter at the Spotted Bear airstrip, so they went to the Spotted Bear Ranger Station just to look around. There had been a huge grocery delivery that day, and the two men watched box after box of food going into the cache. They decided to help themselves to some of it."

"How did they do that? There's always someone at the food cache when it's open," Celie said.

"True, but they waited until night and broke the lock on the door. They really made a mess when they were in there."

Don pointed his thumb at me. "Jessie, do you remember taking pictures after they wrecked the cache? One of your photos showed a partial boot print. It had a distinctive small circle near the tip of the boot. We later matched it to a pair of boots that Doug wore."

"Wow! I'm really glad I took those pictures."

"And there's more. You know the note that Oriole found? The one telling them where to look for the jewels?"

"You mean the one she chewed so badly I could hardly figure out what it said?" I looked at Oriole, who was stretched out by my feet.

"That's the one. Doug and Les had gone fishing and weren't at the Spotted Bear airstrip when Cooter flew in to tell them where the jewels were hidden. It was okay, though, because they had an alternate plan in case the men weren't there when he arrived. He would leave a note for them in their horse trailer parked at the edge of the airstrip. What he didn't know was that the note got wedged into a place where Les and Doug couldn't get it out without tearing it. It tore so badly that all they could read was 'Look in _oo___o_e' and then 'in the____ __house.' So Oriole really didn't damage the note, Jessie."

Mandy laughed as she looked at me. "Oh, so that's why you wanted to look in the woodstove in the bunkhouse that day. It had nothing to do with never having seen a stove like that before."

"Sorry," I said. "That wasn't true, but I had no idea what I was looking for and didn't want to involve you in some wild goose chase."

"Les and Doug had the same problem," Don said. "They thought it was going to be a piece of cake to find the jewels. They rode into Schafer from Spotted Bear and almost ran right into the trail crew."

"So they left the mess on the trail that we had to clean up?" Celie asked. "It's a good thing we didn't catch them in the act. We were all so mad, especially Cody."

"It was their mess all right. And if Oriole hadn't found the meat wrapper with *Schafer* written on it, we might never have made the connection."

Dad pulled his chair back from the table and stretched his legs. "What I don't understand is why Les and Doug set up their tarp at the campground and just sat around the whole time they were there."

"With so many people around they had to look for the jewels when no one would see them going into places where they shouldn't be. That meant spending a lot of time just hanging out, watching. So while the crew was camped out doing trail work, they searched the bunkhouse."

"Oh, no! You mean they're the ones who went through my stuff? They handled my underwear? Eeeww!" Mandy shuddered in disgust. "That really creeps me out!"

"Yeah, but at least you weren't there at the time," Don said. "Jessie wasn't so lucky. The day she went down in the basement of the cookhouse to get a snack, she found the outside door open. Les had waited until no one was around and slipped into the basement through that door. When he heard Jessie upstairs, he didn't have time to go back outside, so he hid under the stairs below a tarp."

"You mean Les locked me in the food cellar?" I asked. "I was sure it was the ghost."

"He's the one who locked you in the cellar, and he's the one who spilled the grain in the grain shed. He thought he might as well help himself to some of that, too—you know— free feed for his horses."

"I'm glad to know Les did it and that I hadn't been sloppy putting the grain away," Jed said.

Don reached down and scratched Casey behind the ears. Casey moaned contentedly and flopped down on the floor.

"That's about it, I guess." Don looked at me. "You know, Jessie, you and Oriole solved this case. If it hadn't been for the two of you we might still be looking for the jewel robbers."

I felt my face redden. "It was really mostly Oriole. She's the one who found the note, helped Casey keep Les and Doug from escaping, and grabbed Hank Cooter before he could get in his plane at Choteau. She was incredible."

Don nodded. "She was, but you're the one who deciphered the note, don't forget. You solved the mystery of the jewel robbery."

I grabbed Oriole and hugged her. "We solved the mystery."

Home

Later that morning, Dad and I sat alone at the kitchen table in the cookhouse. Oriole slept on the floor next to me.

"You know, I'm really proud of you, Jessie," Dad said. "You've come a long way since we left New Mexico. I know how hard it was to leave, but it seems like you're okay with being here at Schafer."

I put my arms around Dad and gave him a big hug. "Leaving New Mexico nearly broke my heart, but all that has changed. I'll always miss my friends there, but everyone here is fantastic, and I love Schafer Meadows and the Great Bear Wilderness. But most of all, I love Oriole. It's hard to think how I ever got along without her."

"She's something all right. She's about as smart as they come. But just being smart doesn't make a good dog. You've worked long and hard with her and have let her become a great dog. The two of you have a relationship that you don't often find."

"I wouldn't have her at all if you hadn't cared enough to worry about me in the first place. Thanks for the best gift ever. I promise to keep working with her so she'll be even better than she is already."

"I don't know how you'll ever do that, but keep trying."

I looked at Oriole and stroked her head while she closed her eyes. "Don said he's really impressed with her. I asked him if Oriole could work with him and Casey to become a law dog. He thought that was a great idea and said we can start the next time he comes to Schafer. And he said I can keep training Oriole during the school year."

I thought for a moment. "You know, Dad, there's still one unsolved mystery. What about the ghost? Do you think there really is one?"

"I don't know, Jessie. We may never have an answer to that one."

I realized it probably wouldn't matter if I never found out about the ghost of Schafer Meadows.

"Dad, thanks for bringing us here. Everything's going to be great."

"I know," he said. He put his arm around my shoulder and smiled. "I know."

The door banged open and Mom burst in. She was beaming, and her eyes, the color of yogo sapphires, shone brightly.

"Come out here now. You've got to see this!"

With that she turned around and hurried out the door. Dad and I looked at each other, shrugged, and followed her.

Mom motioned for us to be quiet as we walked to the edge of the trees by our house. Jed stood staring into the distance. Mom pointed to the airstrip. There on the other side, maybe 200 feet away, was a mother grizzly bear and two cubs. A cloud partially covering the sun caused sunbeams to streak toward the trio. The sun's rays highlighted the mother grizzly's beautiful dark brown coat tipped with silver. The great bear looked in our direction, and we saw her distinctive dish-shaped face as she sniffed the air. The two tiny blonde cubs with light brown legs followed one-by-one behind her as they lumbered along the edge of the airstrip. Too stunned to speak, we watched the mother grizzly raise one paw, revealing claws the size of my fingers. Her powerful shoulder hump moved as she raked a huge log with her claws and rolled it over. The squalling cubs ran up to their mother and the three of them made a feast of ants living under the log.

I looked down at Oriole, who sat motionless by my side, watching the bears with what looked like intense curiosity. Either she was in awe of them or being respectful. It didn't matter—she wasn't about to chase them.

I sat beside her, gathering her to me. She licked my face as we sat in our yard by our home and watched this phenomenal sight.

Life was good!

Bibliography

Historical information about the Spotted Bear and Schafer
Meadows Ranger Stations came from two sources:

McKay, Kathryn L., 1994. *Trails of the Past, Historic
Overview of Flathead National Forest, 1800-1900.* USDA
Forest Service, Flathead National Forest, Kalispell, MT.

Charlie Shaw, 1964. *The Flathead Story*, USDA Forest
Service, Flathead National Forest, Kalispell, MT.

About the Author

Beth Hodder worked for the US Forest Service for over 25 years, almost entirely with the Flathead National Forest in Montana. Part of that time her work took her to the Schafer Meadows Ranger Station in the Great Bear Wilderness, where her husband was a wilderness ranger. A native of Ohio, she and her husband and dog make their home in Montana.

Book Order Form

The Ghost of Schafer Meadows
By Beth Hodder

Ask for *The Ghost of Schafer Meadows* at your local bookstore or order directly from us.

☐ Please send me _____ copies of ***The Ghost of Schafer Meadows*** at $7.99 each plus $3.00 shipping per book.

☐ My check or money order for $_____ is enclosed.

Name_____

Address_____

City/State/Zip_____

Phone Number_____

E-mail_____

Please make your check or money order payable to:

Grizzly Ridge Publishing
Dept. B
PO Box 268
West Glacier, MT 59936

Allow two to four weeks for delivery.